MISSING

Terry nudged Peter's arm. "You asleep?"

"Not anymore I'm not. Where've you been?"

"Looking around. I wanted to make sure I didn't jump to conclusions, let my imagination run wild the way I did last night."

"What are you talking about?"

Terry opened his right fist. Cradled in his palm was a gold hoop and silver butterfly.

"I found this about an hour after you and Judy left for lunch. Tangled up in some grass and dead cattails in the cove."

Peter tried to relax, but he couldn't. There had to be an explanation. The hoop-and-butterfly nose ring was exactly like the one Rebecca wore ... the one she never went anywhere without. The one she was wearing the last time they saw her ...

ONLY CHILD

JESSE OSBURN

AN AVON  FLARE BOOK

ONLY CHILD is an original publication of Avon Books. This work has never before appeared in book form.

AVON BOOKS
A division of
The Hearst Corporation
1350 Avenue of the Americas
New York, New York 10019

Copyright © 1996 by Jesse Osburn
Published by arrangement with the author
Library of Congress Catalog Card Number: 96-96439
ISBN: 0-380-78043-7
RL: 6.0

First Avon Flare Printing: December 1996

AVON FLARE TRADEMARK REG. U.S. PAT. OFF. AND IN OTHER COUNTRIES, MARCA REGISTRADA, HECHO EN U.S.A.

Printed in the U.S.A.

RA 10 9 8 7 6 5 4 3 2

TO NANCY AND GWEN
With all my gratitude

Peter Elton sat at the breakfast table with his mom and dad on the last day of school, and thought about all the wild and wonderful plans he'd made to celebrate his upcoming birthday. Peter and his best friend, Terry Colby, were born in the same hospital—Scarletville General—on the same day—July 15. Terry was the oldest by one hour and twelve minutes, a fact he liked to lord over Peter constantly. Together they'd outlined their party plans in Peter's notebook, along with his history notes and the Latin lessons he despised so much that he'd made only a barely passing grade. But he wasn't too concerned about that now. Report cards didn't come out until one o'clock. By then he'd have thought of a hundred different ways to explain to his parents why he'd failed them and Mr. Dellenberger, his Latin teacher, so miserably.

"We have a surprise for you, darling." Margaret Elton set one of her best china plates, used only for special occasions, on the place mat in front of her son. She'd cooked Peter's favorite breakfast. French toast oozing with low fat margarine, powdered sugar, and homemade strawberry preserves. He should have known, since his mom hated the

1

gooey batter as much as he hated studying Latin, that she was buttering him up for an announcement he wouldn't have guessed in a million years. "Your father's rented a cabin at Sinner's Cove—"

"That's Sinter's Cove," Perry Elton grumbled from behind the *Bledsoe County Times*. "Sinter, Margaret. How many times do I have to tell you?"

"We leave Saturday." She ignored his interruption. "Isn't that wonderful news?"

Peter returned her smile stiffly. Wonderful was not a word he would have used to describe his feelings at the moment. His mother's excitement was a far cry from the disappointment that settled in his stomach like a lump of undigested bread. "What about my birthday?" he asked, in case she'd forgotten.

"Why, we'll celebrate it like we always do, of course." His mom filled his dad's brown mug with coffee and stirred in just the right amount of skim milk.

How long had she been doing that, for pete's sake? Peter's thoughts were momentarily distracted by the small gesture he must have seen a thousand times before but never really noticed until today. Why didn't his dad ever fix his own coffee, or at least pour his wife a cup? He never did anything quite so endearing. Never once, that Peter could remember, had his dad bought her flowers or taken her out to dinner, except when his job demanded it. Heck, he hardly ever talked to her anymore except to criticize her for something unimportant, like serving the same vegetable two nights in a row, or missing an appointment with her hairdresser.

Peter leaned back in his chair and realized with

a pang of guilt why his mother had announced the trip with such zeal. This vacation was going to be the first they'd taken together as a family since Peter was three years old and they'd gone to Disneyland—a trip his father still complained was a waste of time and hard-earned wages. Of course, his dad didn't care much for Christmas, either. Fun was not something Perry Peter Elton III knew how to enjoy.

Still, the revelation that his mother deserved the trip did little to squelch his dashed hopes. He'd looked forward to this birthday like no other before. He and Terry had racked their brains for months, trying to make everything perfect. And all for nothing. Judy would be disappointed, too. She'd probably hand back his class ring when he broke the bad news. Spending the summer alone with his parents was bad enough; breaking up with Judy would be a fate worse than death.

Judy Wand was his girlfriend of six weeks, the best, most exciting month and a half of his life. He'd only been kidding himself about her returning his ring. She'd never do that. Not for something as unavoidable as cancelled plans.

Judy had long black hair, practically down to her waist, and the most incredible jet eyes he'd ever had the good fortune to gaze into up close. She was a great kisser—she'd even taught him a thing or two—but she was so much more, too. Judy was always sweet and genteel, never dull, and a straight A student, the kind of kid most others hated because she never had to study to make good grades. And she was as crazy about Peter as he was about her. She'd said so again last night, just before they'd ended their nightly telephone conversation. Peter had drifted off to sleep with visions of Judy's

3

ebony eyes lulling him into dreams of other mysteries he had yet to discover . . .

Peter and Terry were juniors at Scarletville High School. Judy attended Red Rover, a private school on the other side of town, three blocks from where she lived with her mom and dad in an antebellum-style home large enough for at least a dozen kids. But Judy was an only child, as were Peter and Terry. It was not the only thing they had in common. Judy's birthday was in July too; she'd been born on the seventh, with only a midwife in attendance. It gave them something to talk about when they thought they were being treated unfairly and needed a reason to explain their parents' behavior. Only child, something you couldn't understand unless you were one. Sometimes a blessing, other times a curse. But almost always a built-in excuse when things didn't go your way.

Judy was active in the Roverettes, a flag and drum corps. Only last week she'd been named all-state, an honor bestowed on only two other students in Bledsoe County. And was it any wonder? She was definitely the prettiest girl in Scarletville. At least in Peter's opinion.

"You're going to have a wonderful birthday." His mother nibbled on a slice of bacon, cooked crispy on the edges and raw in the middle, just the way his dad liked. "You'll see." She smiled her most reassuring smile, one that crinkled the tiny lines around her eyes but didn't quite convince Peter that she was telling the truth.

He glanced at the clock above the back door and wondered how long he'd been brooding. He'd have to leave in the next few minutes if he expected to catch a ride with Terry. The lump was still in his

4

stomach. He swallowed hard and tried to hide his disappointment. Bad enough he was going to be separated from Terry on the day they turned eighteen. Being apart from Judy for even one minute, much less the whole summer, made him want to cry, the way he did when he was nine years old and couldn't go to the circus because he had the mumps.

"What'sa matter?" His dad glared at him unexpectedly over the top of the newspaper. The obituaries must have been really boring that morning for him to notice that Peter was in the same room, much less at the same table. "Margaret and I have gone to a lot of trouble planning a summer we thought you'd enjoy. Your last summer at home, I might add."

His mother stifled a small cry. Any mention of her only child going away to college next year always evoked the same response.

"The least you can do is say thank you. For your mother's sake, if not for mine."

"Yes. Of course." Peter looked up, but his dad was concentrating on the newspaper again, the top of his silvery-white hair all that was visible above the headlines. "Thank you, Mother. Thank you, Father." He always addressed his parents formally, the way he'd been taught since infancy.

His first words, spoken from a high chair at this very table, had been "Da-Da." He'd been reminded often how severely he'd been chastised that day and told never again to use the "D word." Those memories, from his earliest childhood, stood out as his most vivid. Right along with the day he'd knocked down a bee hive from the neighbor's tree and had been stung half a dozen times before he could reach the safety of his mother's arms.

"It's just that Terry and I have been planning a party for weeks." He didn't mention Judy, because he could only imagine what his dad would have to say about his so-called love life. "I never dreamed we'd do anything this summer except what we always do. Stay home."

Perry Elton lowered his newspaper and studied his son for signs of insolence. Gratefully, Peter was innocent. This time.

"Terry and I always celebrate our birthdays together." He tried to sound repentant, in case his earlier comments had been misconstrued. "This one's really special, you know. Our eighteenth."

The newspaper went back up and hid his dad's expression before Peter could guess what he was thinking.

"Aren't you and Colby a little too old for birthday cake and balloons?" He spat the words the way he would have a mouth full of bitter coffee.

"It wasn't going to be a theme party." First mistake of the day, letting his mouth get ahead of his brain. Contradicting his father was an unpardonable sin, one punishable in any number of ways. But he couldn't help himself, so he blared on, future consequences be darned. "We were going to order a six-foot submarine sandwich from Darby's, and . . ." Here he paused, gathering up even more courage. "We thought maybe a keg of beer would be nice."

One look from his father told him in no uncertain terms that the day he and Terrence Colby served alcoholic beverages at a party hosted by the Eltons would be the day old Satan served sno-cones in a place called Hades.

"For heaven's sake, Perry." His mother dabbed the corners of her mouth with a linen napkin. "Aren't you going to tell Peter the rest of the news? I think you've teased him long enough."

His father teasing? He hadn't done that since gasoline had cost fifty cents a gallon.

"Why should I, Margaret?" His father had a great, booming voice, especially when he was perturbed. Peter heard his silverware vibrate on the place mat. "Our son seems to think his plans are more important than any you or I could come up with."

"It's a moot point, don't you think?" She spread the napkin in her lap and looked up demurely. "Rather, it will be when you tell him who else is going to Sinner's Cove."

"Sinter, Margaret!" Perry Elton pounded his fist on the table, coffee sloshing onto the walnut finish. "If you realized how foolish you sound when you make the same mistake over and over, you'd stop this instant. I simply will not have our friends thinking I married an uneducated heathen who doesn't know the difference between—"

"Peter, darling," she said, shifting her gaze in his direction.

Peter could only stare at her in stunned silence. Never had his mother cut her husband off in the middle of a tirade.

"There are three other families from Scarletville going to the Cove this summer. The Colbys are one of them."

"Terry?" He couldn't have been more surprised if his mom had told him he'd be sharing a room with the Riley twins, Charlene and Darlene. He and Terry might have been best friends, they might have known each other since kindergarten, but their parents rarely associated unless they attended the same social affair or bumped into each other at a school event. His dad had played in a charity golf tournament with Bob Colby last summer and came home calling him a "drunken jackass." Peter could only imagine what Mr. Colby had told his family over the dinner table that night.

How had they come to plan their summer vacations together? And whose idea had that been? Certainly not his dad's.

"You'll never guess, not in a million years, who else is going." His mother clapped her hands like an excited six-year-old. "The Wands, darling! Judy's parents have rented a cabin not too far from ours."

Unfortunately Peter had just taken a huge bite of French toast and wound up spitting most of it back onto his plate. His dad stared at him, totally disgusted, but didn't say anything. Maybe he knew it was an accident. Or maybe he was just glad Peter had ducked his head in time to keep from splattering him with strawberry jam.

"Judy . . . Judy . . ." He knew he was stammering, but he couldn't help himself. If he'd been shocked about Terry going to Sinter's Cove, he was knocked totally off-kilter by this latest announcement. He and Judy were going to spend the summer together at a romantic lakeside resort? His earlier plans paled in comparison.

His mother leaned back, grinning. "Isn't that just the cat's meow?"

"Yes, Mother." He grinned, too. "Definitely the cat's meow." He glanced at the clock again. Terry was probably waiting out front by the mailbox. In a few more seconds he'd start revving his motor until Peter's dad complained about noise pollution and inconsiderate hoodlums who shouldn't be allowed behind the wheel of a car. Peter pushed himself out of his chair and stopped long enough to kiss his mother's cheek. "Thank you."

The weeks ahead raced through his mind, leaving him slightly dazed and more excited than if he'd just won the lottery. Warm days. Cool nights. Swimming with his best pal. Walking with Judy on a moonlit beach. Suntanning on a blanket, her hair falling back to reveal the skimpiest bikini he'd ever seen . . .

"And you thought we forgot your birthday," Perry Elton mumbled from behind the paper.

"No, sir. Not really." He paused beside his dad's chair, so overfilled with love he was tempted to give him a kiss too. But he figured they'd all had enough surprises for one day. "Thank you. It's going to be a great summer."

His dad mumbled again, something that sounded like, "Gonna help us if it's hot."

Peter grabbed his book bag from a table in the front hall, was out the door and halfway down the porch steps before he realized what his father had really said.

"God help us if it's not."

TWO

One look at his best friend and Peter knew the Colbys had had a similar conversation over breakfast.

"Sinter's Cove," he said as he tossed his bag into the backseat. "Ever been there?"

"Nah." Terry shifted into first gear, squealed the rear tires as he pulled away from the curb. "My old man's idea of a vacation is to drive over to Cavalier City and tour the wineries. He likes the free samples, you know."

Bob Colby was definitely a boozer. But he liked to have fun whether he was drunk or not. Only occasionally did he get inebriated enough to embarrass his family. Peter rarely brought up the subject, and Terry always beat him to it, making some kind of wisecrack to cover up his true feelings.

"So I guess our plans are down the dumper." Terry sped through the residential streets faster than usual, headed toward Jockey Avenue, the quickest route to Scarletville High.

Peter glanced over. Terry was in a bad mood, definitely upset about the announcement. "We'll make new plans. Sinter's Cove will be more fun than anything we talked about."

"For you and Judy, maybe." Terry stared out the windshield, shoulders hunched, his blue cap advertising his dad's car lot pulled low over his forehead, hiding his eyes. His window was rolled down. June breezes whipped around the collar of his red and white windbreaker, which was worn by members of the school track team. "What kind of party is it going to be if none of our friends can be there?"

"It's not that far to Sinter's Cove. We'll invite the same people and maybe some of them can drive up for the day."

Terry took his eyes off the traffic for only a second. "Didn't your folks tell you?"

"Tell me what?"

"No party. At least not like we planned."

It took a moment for the news to sink in. And even longer before a feeling of dread settled over Peter like a rain cloud. He'd been in too big a hurry to leave home; he should have hung around a little longer and asked a few more questions. Obviously his mom and dad had failed to give him all the details.

"What do you mean, no party?"

"No submarine sandwich. No beer. No friends. My old man said he and your dad are taking care of the arrangements this year. They have their own guest list."

"Oh, man . . ." Peter stared out the passenger window, his shoulders slumped against the leather seat. His mom had promised they'd celebrate his birthday, that he'd have a terrific time. He should have realized, should have remembered from past experiences, that her definition of fun was not always the same as his.

11

"What do you think's going on, anyway?" Terry asked.

"What do you mean?" He was so lost in his thoughts, he had no idea what Terry was talking about.

"What did you get for your birthday last year?"

"Clothes, mostly." He'd wanted a computer, but his dad told him he'd have to get a job if he wanted something so extravagant. His mom had sabotaged that idea when she'd said he couldn't go to work until he had straight A's, something they both knew was next to impossible.

"What'd you get the year before?"

"Clothes," Peter replied. "I always get clothes. What's that have to do with anything?"

"Last year I got a key ring with my initials on it." And lost it two weeks later at a track meet in Elmore County. Peter remembered because they'd spent two hours searching for it before Mr. Colby had finally driven from Scarletville with a spare set of keys. "A key ring worth maybe twenty bucks. And this year my folks are treating me to a summer at Sinter's Cove? I'm telling you, buddy, something don't jive."

"Nah." Peter dismissed the comment quickly. Terry was overreacting. "Our folks might be a lot of things. But they usually have our best interests at heart. We'll graduate next year. It's our last summer at home. It's only natural they want to do something special."

"Your last summer, not mine." Terry had already decided that college wasn't for him. He planned to work at Bargainin' Bob's Car Lot and take over the business when his dad retired. Not very ambitious, in Peter's opinion, but he'd never tell his best friend that. Only Terry could decide what kind of future he wanted for himself. "I'm telling you, our parents have ulterior motives for getting us out of town this summer. Why else would they have cooked up such a crazy scheme?"

"Jeez, Terry, aren't you being a little paranoid?" They were silent for a few minutes, until Peter asked, "Who else is going besides you, me, and Judy? Mom said there are four families."

Terry grinned. Peter didn't like the mischievous glint in his eyes. The bad news was going to get worse.

"Dang. Your folks must have made this sound like a whopper of a vacation for you not to ask for details." He rounded the curve so fast, Peter was certain they'd slide into a ditch.

Terry held the steering wheel in a death grip. "LuLu Anderson," he said. "Now ain't that, as your mother would say, the cat's friggin' meow."

"Mom would never say friggin'," was Peter's only response.

He was cleaning out his locker that afternoon, just after lunch, when he sensed someone watching him. He turned and saw LuLu Anderson standing over his right shoulder. Her name was really Lucinda, but somewhere along the way the students at SHS had nicknamed her LuLu.

"Hey," he said uncomfortably. She gave Peter the creeps. Not to be rude, but there was something weird about the way she moved quietly through the hallways, always carrying her Bible on top of her other books, quoting scriptures to anyone who would listen, and some who wouldn't. She had a pasty complexion, a forehead that was constantly broken out in pimples. Thick glasses that magnified her eyes and the kind of brown hair that just hung there, dull and lifeless.

She continued to stand still, watching him for the longest time. So he stopped sorting through papers he hadn't seen since the beginning of the school year and grinned up at her. "How are you, Lu . . . cinda?" He didn't know if she minded being called LuLu or not. Heck, he didn't know anything about her. Till now, this was the longest conversation they'd ever had.

"I'm fine, Peter. How are you?"

"Fine. Great. Never better." His voice quavered. The way she stared at him, he felt she could see into his very soul, know every dirty thought he'd ever had. And he'd had a lot lately, since meeting Judy. "It's a wonderful day, you know." He waited for her to respond, but she didn't. "Last day of school. I'm really happy about that." Why didn't she say something, let him know why she was there? Surely she hadn't come to watch him scrape gum from the bottom of his locker.

"But the path of the just is as the shining light," she said, "that shineth more and more unto the perfect day."

"Huh? Oh. The perfect day. Yeah, I see what you mean."

She smiled. She knew he was lying, and for some reason that seemed to please her. "Mama and Papa told me you're going to Sinter's Cove this summer."

"Yeah. Sinter's Cove. You're going too. It ought to be fun."

"Fun, Peter? Papa's leaving his church in care of an associate pastor for three months. I hardly

14

think he'd make such a sacrifice so I could have a little fun.''

He could only stare at her, slightly dazed and a whole lot confused.

''Like Moses,'' she said, ''I'll be choosing rather to suffer affliction with the people of God, than to enjoy the pleasures of sin for a season.''

''Oh.'' Why bother to go on vacation if not to have fun? And why ruin his before he'd even packed his suitcase?

''I'll see you, Peter.'' She strolled toward her own locker.

''Yeah,'' he said, glad *that* conversation was over. ''See you Saturday.''

''Sunday afternoon.'' She stared at him through thick lenses. ''Papa will preach his final sermon that morning and we'll catch a ride up with Terrence Colby and his family after lunch.''

''Oh . . . man.'' Terry was not going to be happy.

''You've got to be joking!'' They were back in Terry's car, Terry's fingers locked around the steering wheel as if he wanted to choke the life out of it. ''I'm going to be stuck in a car with LuLu Anderson for three hours? I'll be brainwashed by the time I get there. I'll be spouting Bible verses like a lunatic.''

''LuLu's not a lunatic,'' Peter said. Now where had that come from? She wasn't a friend, he didn't look forward to spending the summer with her. But he felt a sudden need to defend her, to try and explain her behavior when he didn't understand it himself.

''Let her ride with you, then.'' Terry had the car

full throttle, racing around corners and through stop signs on what seemed like two wheels. He usually drove over the limit, but never this fast. They were on their way to Red Rover, to a special performance by the Roverettes to celebrate the last day of school. Judy was to be presented her all-state medal shortly after three o'clock, and Peter wouldn't have missed it for the world. WSOE was going to shoot footage for the news at six and ten.

Terry was in a bad mood. The news about LuLu had hit him especially hard.

"I'm telling you, Peter, our parents are out of control. Things are happening that shouldn't be. My old man hasn't been in a church except on the day he got married. Mom doesn't like preachers any more than Dad. They sure as heck wouldn't invite one to ride to Sinter's Cove without a good reason."

"Why do you think?" There had to be any number of reasons why the Andersons and the Colbys had gotten together. To split expenses? To save wear and tear on the Andersons' car? He was only glad it was Terry, and not him, who was going to be stuck with LuLu for two hundred miles. It would be painful, sure. And boring. But he couldn't believe Bob and Virginia Colby were up to anything sinister any more than he suspected his own parents of plotting against him.

"I'm telling you, I got a bad feeling." Terry drove through the entrance of the private school, almost sideswiping the wrought iron gate. "This ain't no ordinary vacation."

"Terry's right," Judy said later as they slid into a booth at Darby's Deli Delights, their favorite hangout. "My parents and I always take the same vacation every summer. There are lots of little shops between Fedder's Point and Charlesburg where Dad buys antiques for his own store. He gets them dirt cheap and triples his money when he re-sells them in Scarletville. He wouldn't pass up that kind of opportunity, not even for a vacation at Sinter's Cove, unless it was very important.''

Peter sat next to her in the booth, watching her as she talked, not paying more than a passing interest to what she had to say. Her hair was spread across her shoulders, so long she had to be careful not to sit on the ends. She'd changed into her school uniform after the performance—navy pleated skirt, white blouse, and red plaid vest—because Red Rover students weren't allowed to leave campus dressed in civilian clothes. More than one guy had turned and stared at her when she'd walked in, and Peter beamed with pride the way he always did when they were together.

"Why the heck are you grinning like a goon?" Terry asked sullenly.

Peter smiled and concentrated on the soft drink that the waitress set before him.

"I'm sorry if you think I'm being silly." Judy touched his hand. "But I know my parents. When they do something unexpected, I can't help but wonder why."

He went over the events in his mind, recalling in only a few seconds everything he'd learned since breakfast. His parents, along with Terry's and Judy's, were taking them to Sinter's Cove for the summer. They'd be there to celebrate their birthdays. Whatever plans they'd made with their friends would just have to be changed. The party wouldn't be what they'd hoped. But they'd have to adjust, wouldn't they? No amount of arguing could change their parents' minds. Least of all his. And what about LuLu Anderson, whom neither of the boys knew very well, and Judy not at all? Somewhere along the way his mom and dad, as well as the Colbys, had become acquainted with Preacher Anderson and his wife, and had failed to mention it to their sons. Nothing sinister about that. Peter didn't tell his parents everything; he imagined they kept secrets of their own, too.

No, for the life of him, he couldn't see why Terry and Judy were trying to find hidden motives, when it was obvious to him that his parents were just trying to make his last summer at home a memorable one. He was defending his parents . . . now wasn't that a twist?

"I think we're going to have a great time," he said, finishing his soft drink. He was expected home in half an hour, and couldn't be late today of all days. His report card was in his hip pocket. Mr. Dellenberger's grade was even worse than expected, so he wanted a chance to talk to his mom first, before his dad came home from the accounting office.

He looked at Terry, cap visor over his eyes, and back at Judy. They were his best friends, the people he cared about most besides his parents. He was glad that they were going to spend the summer together. He was in a great mood, school was out for the summer, Judy was sitting beside him, and nothing anyone said could ruin the plans he'd already begun to make.

Terry slid off the Naugahyde bench and grabbed his keys. "I gotta go."

Peter checked his watch. They still had ten

minutes before they had to leave. "What's your hurry?"

"Gotta go," he said again.

The afternoon ended with a hurried kiss between Peter and Judy outside Darby's, with promises to talk on the telephone later that night if he wasn't grounded from that too. He knew he wouldn't be allowed to go anywhere after his parents saw his report card.

He and Terry rode toward Peter's house in near-silence, his best friend drumming his fingers on the steering wheel in rhythm to the rock music on KJIM. Peter didn't like the mood Terry was in, but he didn't know what to say to draw him out, so he stared past the open window, the wind blowing his hair.

"You're blinded by love, pal."

"What?" He'd been daydreaming, thinking about Judy, and turned toward the driver's seat with a dopey grin.

"Tell me." Terry eased his foot from the accelerator as he rounded the final curve. "How would you feel about Sinter's Cove if Judy wasn't going too?"

"I'd be disappointed."

"Just disappointed?"

"No. More than that, I guess. I'd be upset. Really mad."

"Darn right you'd be mad!" Terry slammed his fist on the dashboard. "You'd ask the same questions Judy and I are asking. You'd want to know what the heck's going on, why our parents are being so generous all of a sudden. As it is . . ." He pulled next to the mailbox and threw the car into neutral. "You couldn't care less that they've

19

planned our entire summer without consulting us first."

For the first time, Peter lost his temper too.

"What's the big deal?" He grabbed his book bag from the backseat and pulled the strap over his arm. "You gotta learn to relax, man. We're going to Sinter's Cove, like it or not. You might as well make plans to enjoy yourself. I have—"

Terry sped away before Peter had an opportunity to slam the door. He climbed the porch steps, his mood dampened, but not completely ruined. Inside, he found his mom in the living room, on the sofa, an orange and white cushion hugged tightly to her chest. She'd been crying, her eyes swollen, mascara ruined.

"Oh." Now what?

He tossed his bag on a wingback just inside the door and sat down on the opposite end of the couch. When his mother finally realized he was in the room, she looked up, startled.

"I didn't hear you come in." She smiled weakly.

"What's the matter?"

"Promise you won't tell your father."

He nodded, his heartbeat slowing down considerably. Whatever the news, it couldn't be too bad. Margaret Elton would never keep anything really important from her husband.

"I've been watching a soap opera," she said. "One of my favorite characters was killed in a mine explosion today. She'd had amnesia for several months, and just before she died, she remembered who she was, and how much she loved her husband and adored her children. Unfortunately, it was too late." She placed the cushion between them and plumped it nervously. "But not a word to your father. He'd never let me hear the end of it if he thought I was addicted to television."

Peter fought the urge to laugh. There was only one TV in the house, a black and white portable in the kitchen, used so infrequently that the cord wasn't plugged in most of the time. His dad hated the racket and said most of the people on television he wouldn't invite into his home anyway. They kept the TV for watching weather reports and an occasional news broadcast. Knowing his mother was hooked on "Days of Our Lives," or some other daytime drama, explained the mood swings she'd experienced lately, the times he'd come home from school to find her teary-eyed and depressed. At least partially. There were other reasons for her sadness, too, he knew. Sometimes at night when he'd climb the stairs to his room, he'd look back to find her staring up at him, all misty-eyed, and Peter knew his mother didn't want him to grow up. Didn't want him to go away to college next year. Another disadvantage to being an only child. Once he was gone, there would be no younger brothers or sisters to fill the void. He could only imagine how lonely his mother would be with Perry Elton for sole companionship.

"I think I'll lie down for a while." She stood, hands buried deep in the pockets of her dress. "Your father called and won't be home until some-time after six. Dinner's ready, it's only a matter of warming it in the oven." She kissed Peter's cheek and left him alone in the living room.

It wasn't until half an hour later, when he was in the kitchen, finishing up a snack of oatmeal cookies and his second glass of milk, that he re-membered his report card. He'd missed the opportunity to discuss Mr. Dellenberger's grade with his mom and would now have to face his dad's wrath at dinner without a mediator. Slumped in the chair, he watched the clock count away the seconds, an ominous reminder that it was not going to be a very pleasant evening in the Elton household.

Ten minutes before six o'clock, he came in from outside, hot and sweaty from mowing the front lawn. He hoped that by doing the chore without having to be reminded, he'd soften the blow of his Latin grade. He poured himself a glass of iced tea, promising himself only a short break. He hadn't yet started on the backyard, so he left the mower in the driveway near the garage door. Switching on the television, he was halfway to the table when he realized there was no picture, no volume. Unplugged. So he trudged back, fished the cord from behind the microwave and fit it into the outlet. Still no picture. No sound, not even static.

He was still fiddling with the buttons and knobs a few minutes later when his dad entered the kitchen through the back door.

"You left the lawn mower in the driveway. I almost ran over it."

No thanks for cutting the grass. No hi, how are you?

His dad was in one of his usual bad moods.

"Judy's going to be on TV," Peter said. "But I can't get the stupid thing to work."

"It hasn't worked in weeks." His dad placed his briefcase on the floor and shrugged out of his suit jacket. "Blew a fuse or something."

"But Mother was . . ." Peter stopped himself just in time. He'd almost spilled the beans about the soap opera.

"Your mother was going to have it repaired," his dad said. "I told her not to bother." He draped his coat on the back of a chair and loosened his tie, the one Peter had given him for Father's Day. "Where's your report card, son?"

Suddenly seeing Judy on the news didn't seem so important anymore. The moment he'd dreaded for weeks was now at hand. There was nothing he could do except go upstairs, get his grades, and carry them back to the kitchen. He lingered beside the cabinet a moment longer, putting off the inevitable as long as possible.

"Well?" His dad's eyebrows arched upward, the way they did just before he lost his temper.

"In my room." He exited through the dining room and went upstairs, trailing his fingers along the banister. His heart pounded, his feet felt as heavy as leaden weights. Jeez, why hadn't he studied harder? Why hadn't he at least prepared his mom and dad when his Latin tests had come back less than perfect? His dad wouldn't see the A's and B's. All he'd notice was Mr. Dellenberger's grade.

He was on his way to his room, heart thrumming in his chest, when he paused outside a door at the end of the hall. This one, always locked, led to another flight of stairs to the attic. That would be a good place to hide until the storm blew over. If only he remembered where his parents kept the key.

He turned at the sound of his mother's footsteps outside her own door.

"Hi." She was wrapped in her favorite robe. "Is your father home?"

"Yes."

She'd been crying again; her eyes were still red and puffy.

"Are you okay?" Peter asked.

"This darn hay fever. It happens every spring. I'd better see to dinner. I fixed your favorite."

His favorite was pizza from Darby's, but he didn't tell her that.

"Hurry now. You know your father hates it when you're late for a meal."

He watched until she turned past the newel post and disappeared into the dining room. There had been no soap opera, no explosion, no favorite character with amnesia.

His mother had lied about the hay fever, too. Unless she'd developed new allergies since last year.

Peter couldn't help but wonder if Terry was right.

Things were happening that shouldn't be.

THREE

Friday morning, a few minutes after his mom left for her weekly appointment with her hairdresser, Peter carried a basket of clean clothes from the laundry room to his bedroom upstairs. He'd not yet begun to pack for his trip to Sinter's Cove, though he'd thought about little else all week, and knew what clothes he planned to take. His dad said he was allowed only one suitcase. Peter sorted through the laundry, still warm from the dryer, and picked out his two favorite T-shirts, baggy khaki shorts, and, of course, his navy blue swimming trunks. From his closet, he grabbed jeans, black trousers, and a white Oxford-cloth shirt for those evenings when he'd have dinner in a restaurant. He moved around his room quickly, from the chest of drawers to the closet and back to the chest again, tossing into his green duffel bag anything he thought he might need—underwear, socks, sandals, leather belt and shoes, another T-shirt, cutoffs, sneakers— though he hoped to spend most of his vacation on the beach, dressed only in his swimming trunks.

Thirty minutes later, by the time he returned downstairs to the laundry room to switch another load from the washer to the dryer, he was even more excited about the trip than before. He only wished Terry and Judy felt the same. Maybe by the time the three of them arrived at the Cove, Judy and Terry would have a change of attitude and the summer would turn out to be as perfect—and romantic—as he had hoped.

The house was especially quiet as he carried the basket to his room and dumped the towels, sheets, and pillowcases onto his bed. The stairs always creaked. But when he was home alone, the boards seemed to moan a little louder, the echoes seemed a little more ominous. He switched on the radio on his windowsill and sang along to the music as he folded towels and sheets and put them away. He sorted through his clothes again, one last time, and picked out more T-shirts, discarded one pair of jeans for another. Finally satisfied that he had the perfect wardrobe, he went to the bathroom, gathered up his toiletries, and stuffed them in his duffel bag. He was nearly finished when he noticed the busted zipper. The last time he'd used the canvas bag was on a Boy Scout camp out, five, six years ago. Since then it had been stashed on the top shelf of his closet, out of sight and forgotten.

Muttering, though he refused to let his anticipation be ruined by a lousy broken zipper, he went in search of another suitcase. There was no luggage in the hall closet, nothing downstairs in the basement or outside in the garage. Ten minutes later, he knew there was only one other place to look. Upstairs. In the attic. He hadn't been there since . . . since he was four or five years old, too young to remember much about the place except the dusty corners and cobwebs strung along the rafters.

He found the key, of all places, beneath the

kitchen sink on a nail, almost out of reach. He wasn't even sure it was the right key until he raced to the attic door, taking the stairs two at a time, and slipped the key into the lock. The door swung open on rusty hinges. The first thing he noticed— just like the last time he'd been here—was the dank smell that wafted down the narrow flight of stairs.

For reasons he didn't understand, he hesitated before going up. The attic was unchartered territory, though it was part of the house he'd lived in all his life. His parents had never told him the uppermost floor was off-limits. But there were some rules, he knew, that didn't need to be spelled out in detail. This was where his mom and dad kept their most cherished possessions. There was nothing of great monetary value, but the door was kept locked, the key protected. Still, he needed a suitcase. And the attic seemed the only logical place to look.

The light switch was just inside the doorway, to his right. The wooden stairs went up four risers and turned sharply left. The bare bulb above the landing cast more shadows than light; dust motes danced in the gray haze like dirty snow. There was no handrail so Peter climbed upward, his fingers braced against the wall. There were reasons why his parents were so protective of the junk up here, though at present, nothing he thought of made much sense. He wished he'd remembered to bring a flashlight. The light in the attic was even more dim than in the stairwell. All the bulbs were burned out except for one, in the far left corner, almost hidden behind a stack of wooden crates marked NURSERY—TOYS—BABY CLOTHES. He worked his way past discarded furniture, lamps, and gardening tools strewn haphazardly, blocking the aisle. Dust was everywhere, so thick he could feel it collecting in his nostrils like soot. The nearer he came to the back wall, the more cloying the smells became. Whatever his parents had stored up here had gotten wet and mildewed over the years. He wouldn't mention that to his dad, though. He wanted to spend his vacation at Sinter's Cove, not reshingling the roof.

He felt odd, and a little nervous, as he searched the shelves for a suitcase. As if he'd entered someone else's house, and the junk stashed here belonged to some other family. Most of the stuff he couldn't remember seeing before, though a lot of it was marked BABY-this and BABY-that. He must have really been spoiled as a newborn and toddler. One of the advantages of being an only child, he supposed. Though somewhere along the line, his mom and dad decided moderation was more suited to their son, so his toys and clothes had been stored in wooden crates, the lids nailed tight. His crib and other nursery furniture were stacked against the wall, partially covered in drop cloths splattered with pastel paint.

He wondered . . . Would he get in trouble if he pried open a lid? Just one, to satisfy his curiosity?

First things first, he decided. He located an old suitcase, covered with dust, without too much trouble. He carried it to the door and placed it at the top of the stairs. His mom would be home soon, just about any minute, and he didn't want to be caught up here. If his parents asked about the suitcase, he'd tell them he found it in the garage. It was only a small lie. They probably wouldn't remember this piece of luggage any better than he did, much less where it had been stored for the past umpteen years.

He reentered the attic. This time he moved along the aisles slowly and took in the room's contents with a little awe and a whole lot of curiosity. He slid several boxes out of the way so he could see behind them. Some were heavy, others so light he could handle them with one hand. All of them taped and clearly labeled. He sat on the floor, so cramped for space his legs would barely fit, and cradled one of the smaller boxes in his lap. BABY'S ROOM—MISCELLANEOUS. He tore open the tape and peered inside. Nothing as interesting as he'd hoped. Blue, white, and pink blankets. Cloth diapers that were dingy gray. All kinds of cute little outfits in varying sizes. LITTLE SLUGGER was emblazoned across a striped shirt with matching blue shorts and a baseball cap so small it could have fit a doll. At the bottom of the box were a couple of dresses. One white with lots of frills, the other pink with a lace collar. He hoped he'd never worn one of those. They'd probably been given to his mom before he was born, before the Eltons had been blessed with a son.

He replaced the tape as best as he could and reached for another box. Nothing inside this one either except clothes and baby bottles, the nipples stored in a plastic bag. Boring. For the most part. Except it was kind of fun to have a part of his past revealed. He had no conscious memory of wearing any of these clothes or playing with any of the toys. He'd no doubt been a toddler when they'd been carried upstairs. He wondered . . .

His eyes scanned the boxes, took careful note of the labels. BABY'S ROOM. BABY CLOTHES.

Not PETER'S ROOM or PETER'S CLOTHES. He wondered if his parents had wanted to have another child, if that's the reason his mom saved all this stuff. He couldn't imagine a brother or sister. Though once, before he was old enough to start school and didn't have anybody to play with, he'd wished for nothing else. That was about the same time he thought he might be adopted and snuck up here one day while his dad was at work and his mom was outside in her garden to search for his adoption papers. He hadn't gotten very far in his hunt before his mom caught him and smacked him a couple of times on his bottom on their way back downstairs. He'd never seen her so upset. When he explained what he was doing, her anger dissipated, and she'd hugged him to her chest. He couldn't remember what she'd said, only that he felt better, and quickly forgot the idea that anyone other than Perry and Margaret Elton were his bio-logical parents.

A charley horse worked its way through his right thigh, so he stood, and listened for any noise down-stairs. He thought he could probably hear his mom's car when she pulled into the drive. But, honestly, he'd been so caught up reminiscing, the Roverettes could have marched through the living room and he might not have noticed. He wasn't ready to leave yet. This place was like a museum or a toy store. There was too much to explore in a short while.

He found a faux leather chest shoved against the back wall, its clasp bound securely with a padlock. He tugged on it, he could probably search the house over and never find the key, and was surprised when the metal rivets were so old and rusted that they slid out with very little effort. Inside, these contents were more interesting. Books of poetry tucked inside the folds of an old quilt. A lace tablecloth and napkins wrapped in tissue. Near the bottom, beneath a stack of home and garden magazines dated from before he was born, was a photograph album with a faded red binder and gold letters. Peter carried the book to the north wall, to the only window in the attic, and tilted it toward the sunlight to have a better look. The cover was frayed, the letters turned to burnished copper.

He thought he remembered the album. Maybe downstairs in the living room on the shelf where his dad kept his favorite western novels, or on the coffee table next to the arrangement of silk roses. Or maybe . . . Maybe he'd run across it, that day years ago when he'd hunted for his adoption papers. He remembered the album, but not what was inside. He hoped there were photos of grandparents he'd never met. Aunts, uncles, cousins—family his parents never talked about.

Packing for vacation was forgotten as he flipped to the first page, to a black and white photograph of his parents. His dad stood behind his wife's left shoulder, a baby with wavy hair and thick, curling eyelashes cradled in his mom's lap. He thought he saw some semblance to himself now. Though his hair was straight, his lashes not so long. He'd been young in this picture. Not more than a few weeks old.

He'd turned to the second page, an 8 × 10 of him taken a year later, when his hair was straight, his eyelashes as sparse as they were now, when he heard footsteps at the bottom of the stairs. He was too shaken up to think rationally, to put the album back where he'd found it. Instead, he turned to the wall behind him and dropped the book in an opening below the window. The red binder fell completely out of sight between the Sheetrock and jack studs.

"Peter, what are you doing up here?"

She stood in the doorway a minute later, her face and long hair half-hidden in shadows.

"Darn, Judy."

Thank goodness it wasn't his mom.

"You just about scared the daylights out of me." He was grounded from the telephone and hadn't talked to her or Terry since the last day of school.

She moved toward him and glanced around as awestruck as he had been earlier. "What are you doing up here?"

He gestured at the suitcase near her feet. "Getting ready for my trip. What about you? All set to go?"

She shrugged. "I suppose."

"Don't tell me you're still not excited about Sinter's Cove." He joined her at the door. With the suitcase in one hand, the other wrapped around Judy's waist, he escorted her downstairs. The landing was so cramped, there was not enough room for them to walk side by side.

"You know, Peter, you're not a very good liar. You were doing something you're not supposed to do. What?"

He shrugged and hoped he appeared as nonchalant as she had. "I told you, looking for a suitcase." He didn't feel like explaining, even to Judy, that parts of his own home were off-limits. And he sure didn't want to admit he'd been so scared by her sudden appearance that he'd lost one of his mom's photo albums behind a wall.

"What are you doing here?" he asked. "You know I'm not allowed to see you until we get to Sinter's Cove."

"I saw your Mom at Miller's Supermarket a few minutes ago. She went in just as I came out, so I knew she'd be there long enough for me to stop by and say hello."

"I'm glad you did." Peter placed the suitcase outside his bedroom door and joined Judy downstairs in the entrance hall. "I've missed you these last couple of days."

"I missed you, too. Terry's not nearly as much fun to talk to as you."

"Terry?" His mouth went dry and he didn't know why. "You've been talking to Ter?"

"Last night. And the night before." She opened the door so she could watch the street in case his mother came around the corner.

Peter was jealous of other guys, sure. But never his best friend. Terry wouldn't make a move while Peter was homebound, unable to defend himself. They'd never shown interest in the same girls, their tastes were too varied. Except Judy was an exception. What guy wouldn't go after her, given the chance? Even a close friend.

"We're still trying to figure out our parents' sudden generosity," she said as she stepped onto the porch. "What this trip is all about."

Jealous thoughts still raced through his brain and he was too confused to continue an argument he thought they'd settled the other day.

Instead, he concentrated on Judy. The way the sunlight streaked through her dark hair. She looked as beautiful as always, in tight jeans and a denim blouse.

"I'd better go before your mom catches me." She paused at the bottom of the steps and smiled up at him, her eyelashes as thick as the baby's picture he'd seen in the attic. "I wouldn't want to get you into any more trouble."

"I'll see you at the Cove, I guess." He leaned against the rock pilaster as visions of Judy in a bikini flashed through his mind as vivid as any movie he'd watched at Scarletville Cinema. "We'll have all summer to be together."

"Ummm." She stopped before she reached her car, which was parked beside the mailbox. "Tell me, Peter. The pictures you were looking at. Who were they of?"

So he hadn't been quick enough. Judy had reached the attic in time to see the album.

"Me. As a baby."

"I'd like to see them sometime."

"I'll show you mine if you'll show me yours."

She grinned, continued toward the curb. "I'll have to ask Mom first. I'm not even sure she has any pictures of me as a baby."

He watched her drive away and wondered if it were possible that the Wands were even less sentimental than his own mom and dad. What parents in their right mind wouldn't have snapshots and photographs scattered throughout the house chronicling the growth of their only child? Especially a daughter as gorgeous as Judy.

FOUR

Saturday morning, only a few minutes behind schedule, Peter carried his suitcase downstairs and placed it in the foyer next to his mom's and dad's luggage. His parents were in the kitchen, his dad no doubt upset that Peter was late for breakfast. His mom served platters of bacon, scrambled eggs, and toast in her usual good mood, though this morning she hummed her favorite song, slightly off-key. Her voice filled the room and Peter smiled as he slid into his chair across the table from his dad.

Perry Elton lowered his newspaper and stared at him over the headlines. He wasn't exactly grinning, but it was a good start.

"All packed, son? Ready to go?"

His father never greeted him in the morning, much less instigated a conversation. Peter was tempted to pinch himself to make sure he wasn't dreaming.

"Yes, sir. One suitcase, just like you said."

"I checked the weather forecast. There's not the slightest chance of rain through Monday." Perry Elton winked at his wife and slid the paper back up to cover his expression. "Looks like we'll have clear sailing all the way to Sinter's Cove.''

The next surprise came an hour later, after the breakfast dishes had been put away and all the appliances unplugged in case of an electrical storm while they were away. Peter and his dad loaded the car while his mom bustled through the house, ran upstairs and down, double-checked window locks and made sure she hadn't overlooked any last-minute details. Finally, just before ten o'clock, while Peter closed the trunk lid, his dad went inside and escorted his mom out with gentle assurances that everything would be okay, that the neighbors would look after the place while they were gone. Peter didn't blame his mom for worrying. His dad had, over the years, insulted everyone in the neighborhood at least once.

The dead bolt slid into place and a moment later his parents strolled toward the car, hand in hand, his dad dressed in white linen trousers and a coral button-down shirt. His mom wore a yellow sundress and carried a straw hat tied with sunflower ribbon. His dad said something Peter couldn't hear and his mother giggled, the lilt of her laughter the most beautiful sound Peter had heard in a long time.

He couldn't help but feel good about the trip. The summer stretched ahead with limitless possibilities. Heaven knew his parents deserved a vacation. He only hoped that somewhere across town, Judy was having the same thoughts; and that tomorrow, when Terry drove away with his folks and LuLu Anderson, he wouldn't behave like a corpse on his way to the cemetery.

Peter reached for the door handle, about to climb

into the backseat, when his dad tossed him the keys.

"I thought you might like to drive, son."

He was almost certain he was dreaming now. His dad never let him drive in town, much less on the Interstate.

"Well, are you going to stand there all day?" His dad slid into the front passenger seat. "Or are we going to blow this one-horse town?"

"Perry, dear, did you remember to pack your blood pressure medicine?" his mother asked.

"Yes."

"Did you stop delivery on the newspaper?"

"Yes, dear."

"Did you call the phone company—"

"It's taken care of, Margaret. Stop worrying."

Peter glanced over, just to make sure his dad wouldn't start to criticize him the moment he put his foot on the accelerator. But he was studying a state map, following with his finger the route he'd outlined with a yellow marker. Peter felt beads of sweat on his forehead, his fingers were numb, and he wasn't even out of the driveway yet. He was positive he'd have a wreck if he didn't relax. He made it past the neighborhood, took a shortcut to avoid downtown traffic, and drove onto the entrance ramp without so much as a word from either of his parents. His mom's window was rolled down, the breeze not strong enough to combat her heavily sprayed hairstyle.

His dad seemed especially relaxed. If he was still mad at Peter for failing Latin, he certainly gave no indication. He'd refolded the map and placed it in his briefcase though he made no effort to bury himself in his work the way Peter expected.

They rode in silence for ten, fifteen miles. Finally, Peter pushed the cruise control button and fell in with the rest of the traffic travelling just below the speed limit.

"Will it distract you, son, if I play the radio?" his dad asked.

"No, sir. Not at all." His dad was asking his permission?

"What's your favorite station?"

"KJIM 103.4," his mom answered from the back seat. "He listens to it all the time at home."

"It's rock," Peter warned them. "If you'd rather listen to something else."

His dad glanced over his shoulder, smiled at his wife. "Our son thinks we're old fogeys, Margaret. He thinks we can't appreciate modern music."

"No, sir," Peter started to apologize immediately. "I didn't mean—"

"Relax, son. I'm a Beatles fan from way back. I even wore my hair long before it was fashionable." He turned the dial, found KJIM, and set the volume at a comfortable level. "How's that, Margaret? Can you hear back there?"

"Yes, dear. Thank you."

Peter glanced in the rearview mirror, watched as a Greyhound bus pulled into the passing lane and swept past, its loud motor drowning out further conversation. He wondered if he were living a scene from a horror movie. Someone had broken into his house last night and replaced his parents with pod people.

The next surprise came at twelve minutes past noon when his dad pointed at a road sign and told Peter to take the next exit. Peter was glad for the break; he was just about to suggest it himself. Not yet in desperate need of a men's room, he was awfully close.

The truck stop, with its orange metal roof, was located north of a four-way stop at the end of the ramp. The parking lot was crowded. A group of patrons waited outside the double doors to be seated in the dining room.

Peter offered his dad the keys once he'd angled the Mercedes between the yellow lines.

"Keep 'em, son. Unless you're tired of driving."

"No, sir. I'm fine."

Judy and her parents were inside, in a corner banquette overlooking the parking lot.

Margaret Elton and Mona Wand greeted each other like old friends. Peter's dad shook Mr. Wand's hand and even slapped him on the back before he slid into the booth beside his wife.

Peter watched them incredulously. Judy, he knew, was as shocked as he was.

"I didn't know you were going to be here," he told her.

She smiled, swept her long hair over one shoulder. "You're the last person I expected to see, too." She took his hand, told her parents she had to go to the restroom, and walked with Peter to the end of the crowded dining room.

Only when they were out of sight of their parents did she kiss him, lightly, on the cheek.

"You're right, Peter. I think it's going to be a great summer. My mother and I have talked more in the last couple of hours than we have in the past six months. She asked all kinds of questions—not poking in my business, mind you—she just wanted to know what's going on in my life. How's school?

How're my friends? My dad and I even talked about you."

"What'd you say about me?" He grinned the way he always did when he was with Judy.

"Wouldn't you like to know?" she said as she closed the restroom door behind her.

More than an hour later they were back in the car, on their final leg to Sinter's Cove. The Wands, in their silver and gray van, followed the Eltons for the remainder of the trip. Judy was seated directly behind her dad, so Peter couldn't see her. But he didn't mind. They'd reach the Cove in less than an hour. After that, he and Judy would have all summer together.

As anxious as Peter was to reach the resort, he was almost sorry when he exited off the Interstate and followed a blacktop around the side of Wild Horse Mountain. He and his parents kept up a lively conversation after they left the restaurant. They talked about everything from politics to sports to Peter's plans for his last year of high school. His mother grew teary-eyed, so he'd gotten off that subject and on to another as quickly as possible. He talked about his friends, Terry and Judy, mostly. He mentioned Terry's comment about spouting Bible verses after being locked in the car with LuLu Anderson. His dad laughed so hard that his mother chastised him for making fun of good Christian people. She'd drifted to sleep ten minutes later, her head resting on a satin pillowcase so she wouldn't muss her hair. Peter glanced at her in the mirror as they followed the winding road down the other side of the mountain. His heart was filled with good memories. For all their strictness, and their aloofness sometimes, he had no doubt that his folks loved him and wanted only the best for their son. He was growing up. This time next year he'd be making plans to leave home for good.

"You realize, son." His dad's voice grew suddenly serious. "The same rules apply here that apply at home."

Peter nodded, though secretly he'd hoped he'd be given a little more freedom this summer. Not that he'd do anything his parents wouldn't approve of; just because he was on vacation didn't mean he couldn't be grounded.

"You and Judy will be together every day," his dad said as they turned onto a gravel road. The Wands were directly behind, almost lost in a cloud of dust. "I expect you to behave like a gentleman."

"Yes, sir."

"You'll have a curfew, just like always."

"Yes, sir."

White rail fences lined both sides of the road. Ahead, to the left, a row of poplar trees marked the entrance to Sinter's Cove, though the resort itself was not yet in view. Peter glanced in the rearview mirror again. Judy leaned forward in her seat and peered between her parents' shoulders. Afternoon sunlight glistened off her ebony hair.

"Oh." Peter's mom roused from her nap. "We're almost there?"

His dad glanced over his shoulder. "Very close, dear."

Peter expected his mom to be happy . . . excited. But she rested her head on the pillow and closed her eyes without comment.

"Turn right, son, across that cattle guard," his dad said.

He obeyed without hesitation. There were no signs to indicate the way and he would have gotten lost on his own. He wondered how his dad was so familiar with the area. But he realized a moment later that this was his dad, after all—Perry Elton never did anything halfheartedly. He'd no doubt charted their course without the slightest risk of getting lost. He'd probably even called ahead and asked for specific directions. If there was one thing his dad hated most, it was not knowing where he was going or how to get there. He mapped out his own life as carefully and conscientiously as he did his only son's.

The final entrance to Sinter's Cove Resort was marked by a rustic wooden gate, held open by a log chain wrapped around a rock column. The name was spelled out in cedar branches across the top, the letters dappled in sunlight and shadows as they drove through.

Peter had dreamed of Sinter's Cove ever since his parents' surprise announcement. He'd tried to imagine, especially at night as he lay in bed and stared at the ceiling, what their accommodations would look like. He expected a series of one and two-bedroom cabins with a porch and maybe even a swing. He'd hoped they'd be right on the lake, or at least just a short walk away.

"I didn't know it would be so . . ." His mom was awake again. This time she leaned toward the window as she tried to take in the panoramic view. "I didn't expect anything quite so luxurious. Are you sure we can afford this?"

Peter expected his dad to be insulted, to lose his cool and lecture his mom on how hard he worked and how their finances were none of her concern, but instead he half-turned in his seat, as far as his shoulder strap would allow.

"You like, Margaret? Peter? Think you can rough it out here for a couple of months?"

The cabins in the distance were more like two-story condominiums large enough to accommodate three or four families. The outside walls were covered with red brick and rough cedar. Leaded windows stretched from floor to ceiling and mirrored evergreen, oak, and elm trees along the gravel paths.

"There's the office." His dad pointed the way.

Peter almost missed the U-shaped drive; he was too busy trying to locate Lake Andrew Sinter. The clubhouse was three times as large as Judy's house, with dormer windows and red brick walls covered in ivy. The porte cochere served as a trellis for roses and ivy.

Peter parked the car and was standing outside before his mom and dad had a chance to unfasten their seat belts.

There was a doorman, dressed in white linen and gold epaulets, at his side.

"Welcome to Sinter's Cove." He was older than Peter's dad, with gray hair and a neatly-trimmed mustache. "I hope you had a good trip."

"Fine. Thank you." Peter walked to the back of the car, too awestruck to pay close attention to anyone. Even Judy was momentarily forgotten until she slipped her arm through his.

"Isn't this place terrific?"

"I hope Terry thinks so."

"It must be costing our folks a fortune."

"I wonder if our cabins are close together." Hand in hand, they walked to a water fountain and fishpond at the end of the drive. "What's the first thing we're going to do?" Peter was over his shock and anxious to get their vacation officially under way.

"I bought a really great bikini." Judy smiled and squeezed his fingers. "I can hardly wait for you to see me in it."

He didn't mean to leer, but his imagination conjured up images of Judy in sexy swim wear, and he couldn't help himself. It seemed an eternity before his dad and Mr. Wand exited the lobby, each with a key to their cabins.

The Wands were in number 4, a short walk from the clubhouse, restaurant, and coffee shop, while Peter's family was closer to the lake, in number 17. The Colbys' and Andersons' cabins were side by side, separated from the golf course by a white picket fence.

"If we hurry," Perry Elton said to Judy's dad, "we'll have time to introduce ourselves to the pro before Happy Hour."

"Find the lake," Judy said. "I'll meet you there in half an hour."

"Why so long? It takes thirty minutes to get into a bikini?"

She winked. "It'll be worth the wait." And went to join her parents in the van.

The drive to their cabin proved to be a little more slow going than Peter had expected. The roads were narrow and bumpy; recent rains had washed out deep ruts. He dodged them as best he could, was careful not to drag the muffler along the way.

"Joe and I are off to the course," his dad said. "What do you have planned, Margaret?"

"Mona was nice enough to let me drop an ice

44

chest at her house this week because they have room in the van and we don't. The least I can do is help her put away her groceries.''

Joe and Mona? His parents were already on a first name basis with Judy's folks?

There was no further discussion until after Peter had parked under a shady tree and walked to the back of the car to unlock the trunk.

"I don't suppose you and Judy want to help, Peter?''

"Don't be ridiculous, Margaret.'' His dad's thunderous voice had taken on a gentler quality since they'd departed Scarletville. "Surely you remember what it's like to be young. To want to spend time alone with someone your own age.''

"Yes. Of course I remember.'' She switched her straw hat to her right hand and wrapped the other around her husband's waist. She looked happy and vibrant, more at ease than she had in years. His dad's silvery-white hair glistened in the afternoon light, the strands that were always so carefully coiffured blown awry by warm breezes. For once, he made no effort to hide his receding hairline. "As much as I dreaded coming here, Perry, I must admit you've outdone yourself. Sinner's Cove is a paradise—''

"Sinter, Margaret. Try and remember for my sake, won't you?''

Peter unloaded the luggage, his suitcase first, as his parents set off along the path to the porch. His mom hummed a sweet song, and his dad hurried alongside her, trying to keep step with her eager pace.

Peter knew now where he'd gotten that dopey

grin whenever he looked at Judy. He'd inherited it from his dad.

Terry Colby lay across his bed that evening, just after dark, and listened as his parents argued in another part of the house. His old man had arrived home late from the country club where he'd played a round of golf with his buddies. He'd no doubt spent more time at the bar than he had on the greens. Though he couldn't hear what was said, Terry knew his dad's speech was slurred, his mom's voice so full of venom that she had little difficulty stating her opinions.

He hated when his folks argued and they'd done it a lot lately. His dad was drinking more and more and his mom was tolerating it less and less. Sometimes he wished he weren't an only child, that he had a brother or sister to help him through the rough times. But fortunately, he had the best friend in the whole world. Expect Peter was already at Sinter's Cove, probably with Judy, having the time of his life.

Terry slammed his fist into his pillow, covered his head, and tried to shut out his parents' voices. They were going from room to room, shouting at each other. His mom was angry enough to throw dishes, pots and pans, anything she could get her hands on. These little altercations hadn't grown into anything physical, but Terry figured it was only a matter of time.

Nights like these he wished they'd file for divorce and get it over with. Why'd they hang around and make each other miserable? Not for his sake, he hoped. Right now he'd welcome the peace and quiet.

Terry squeezed his eyes closed and tried to concentrate on the white lights that twinkled like stars. His folks had moved from the kitchen to the dining room; he could no longer hear his mother's angry shouts batter against his closed door. Her voice was muffled. She was, he guessed, in tears by now.

He had hoped Peter might be right, that this surprise vacation their parents arranged would be the start of something different. He'd tried to voice his doubts—even explain them as best he could—but his best friend was so blinded by love, he couldn't see anything except visions of Judy Wand in a bikini.

His dad was shouting again. Terry was tempted to call the resort, hold up the telephone so his buddy could hear the commotion.

"Yeah, pal," he'd say. "Mom and Dad certainly have my best interests at heart. Sure, they want to make my summer before graduation extra special. That's why I'll be lucky if they don't kill each other and I wind up an orphan before the night's over."

Suddenly, the yelling stopped. His dad no longer cursed, his mom no longer wept. The storm was over, all that was left to face was the aftermath.

Terry sat on the edge of the bed and prepared himself for Round Two. Moments later, he heard his dad's footsteps outside his bedroom door.

"Ter, ole buddy, you awake?" He opened the door just a crack, but didn't turn on the light. "How's my little slugger?"

"Not so little anymore. Dad, I'm almost eighteen." He was angry and needed to do a little shouting of his own.

"Umm . . . guess you heard."

"Guess I did. Right along with the neighbors."

"Hey, listen." His dad leaned against the door frame to steady his balance. "Your mom's already mad at me. Don't you be, too."

"I hope you didn't drive home," Terry said, not ready to be so forgiving yet.

"Nope." His dad shook his head and staggered to the left. "Caught a ride with the good Reverend Anderson. Sucker plays a mean round of golf."

"You got drunk in front of a preacher?" Terry could only imagine what LuLu would have to say about that tomorrow.

"You should 'a been there." His dad tried not to slur his words. Tried so hard it was almost comical. "He matched me drink for drink. The problem is, he holds his liquor better'n me."

So LuLu's old man had downed a few of his own, huh? She'd better not say one word or Terry would cram her holier-than-thou attitude down her stupid throat.

His dad weaved across the room and sat on the edge of the bed. "Your mom said you went to bed early, to get rested up for the trip tomorrow."

"Yeah," he lied. The truth was, he wanted to be alone, to try and figure out why he couldn't get excited about going to Sinter's Cove. He tried to look at the vacation from Peter's point of view. But it was no use. Their parents had ulterior motives. He could see that, even if his best friend couldn't.

"What would you say if I told you we weren't going?" his dad asked. "Would you be disappointed?"

"Hell, no."

"Don't cuss, son. Your mom wouldn't like it. And she's mad enough already."

48

"Mad enough she cancelled the vacation?"

His dad didn't answer for so long that Terry was positive he hadn't heard the question. Bargainin' Bob Colby leaned forward on the mattress, hands between his knees, and stared at the carpet. There was very little light in the bedroom. Terry's curtains were closed. Just a small triangle fell through the open doorway. Enough to show his dad's bloodshot eyes and down-turned mouth.

"How'd you feel about going off on our own, just the two of us?" his dad asked finally. "We could go fishing at Camp Hudgens, or hike to the top of Wild Horse Mountain and camp out for a couple of weeks."

Terry felt his melancholy mood slip away. This was the kind of trip he expected his dad to come up with. Not some fancy resort where they'd be forced to share their time with a bunch of strangers. He only wished Peter were home, that he'd forego any plans at Sinter's Cove, and traipse off into the wilderness with him and his dad. That, in Terry's opinion, was the only way to make this summer one they wouldn't forget.

He was just about to respond, to tell his dad no way would he go without inviting Peter first, when he noticed his dad wiping his nose with his shirt sleeve. He'd been so wrapped up in his thoughts, excited by the prospect of rearranging his summer, that he didn't realize his dad had begun to cry.

The spell was broken. Whatever plans the old man had come up with were pipe dreams. His dad rarely got drunk enough to cry in his beer, but when he did, the binges could go on for hours.

He was almost relieved when his mom showed up at the door. She'd taken a shower and washed her hair, her tangled red curls just a shade or two lighter than her husband's and son's. She wore no makeup and her favorite chenille robe—pink with red roses—her shoulders slumped beneath the heavy fabric. She was no longer angry; merely exhausted, too tired to continue a battle that had waged on for years.

"Think you can help me get him to bed?"

"Ain't going to bed," his dad said. "I'm goin' fishing . . . taking my son fishing."

With Terry on one side and his mom on the other, they lifted Bob Colby from the bed, and struggled with him toward the door. Most of his weight was on Terry's shoulder and they nearly stumbled a time or two.

"We leave at daybreak, son," his dad said. His breath reeked of liquor and Terry turned away to avoid the fumes. "First light. Fishin'. Campin'. I'm still the head of this household and I say pooh on Sinter's Cove."

"Yeah, Dad. Whatever."

They reached the end of the corridor, his parents' bedroom, and Terry waited at the threshold until his dad was on his side, wrapped like a mummy in the floral comforter. His mom unlaced his shoes and dropped them beside the chest of drawers.

"I can handle it from here," she said. "You'd better go back to bed and rest up for tomorrow."

"Fish a' biting, son," his dad mumbled. "Gotta leave early."

It was only nine o'clock. Terry was too keyed up to sleep. But his room seemed the best place to retreat to right now. So he went back and closed the door behind him.

He stretched out, hands behind his head, and

stared at the ceiling. Camp Hudgens or Wild Horse Mountain wasn't such a bad idea. He was tempted to sneak out, leave his parents a note. Peter would be peeved. But he'd get over it in a day or two. He'd have Judy to keep him company.

Camp Hudgens would be crawling with youth groups this time of year. He'd been there once, back in third grade, and he knew the busiest season was the first month after school let out for the summer. He'd been so young then, he'd been more interested in rock formations and learning how to use his Swiss army knife than he had been in girls.

But things were different now. He was older. Wiser. Sneaking off to Camp Hudgens made a heck of a lot more sense than riding three hours with LuLu Anderson, watching his best friend ogle Judy Wand, and wonder why his parents were so hellbent on getting him to Sinter's Cove in the first place.

Yeah. Camp Hudgens. He mind still reeled with plans when he drifted to sleep an hour later.

FIVE

Peter paced from one end of the wooden porch to the other, his footsteps muffled by his favorite pair of sneakers. Judy lounged in a wrought iron chair, her long hair tied with a ribbon, yellow bikini covered with a short terry cloth robe. She'd been tolerant for well over an hour, not saying a word as Peter walked in front of the rails and glanced at his watch every five minutes, but he knew she was about to reach the end of her patience. She wanted to wait for Terry near the pier, her favorite stretch of beach, and Peter had agreed at first, expecting his best friend to arrive no later than three or four o'clock. But it was close to five-thirty and there was still no sign of the Colbys.

He checked his watch again, stepped aside of the clubhouse door to avoid being hit. The doorman, dressed in white linen and gold epaulets, hurried down the wooden steps to greet new guests as they parked their station wagon at the end of the circular drive.

"It doesn't matter whether you're here or not." Judy stretched, her arms and legs slightly burned from the hours she'd spent stretched out on a quilt after lunch. "Terry's going to be in a rotten mood.

We should at least try and have fun before he gets here."

She was right. The second day of their vacation was almost over and he hadn't been able to enjoy himself—not very much anyway—for fear that Terry was miserable, stuck in the car with LuLu Anderson. He couldn't explain how he felt, wasn't even sure he understood himself, but he'd feel disloyal if he weren't there to greet Terry the minute he arrived. His best friend, he knew, would do the same for him.

"I hope you're not going to be like this all summer." Judy walked to the end of the porch, stood beside Peter, and rested her elbows on the cedar rails. "Terry's a big boy. He can take care of himself."

"Yeah. I know. But—"

"We told the others we'd be back in time to take a swim before dinner."

They'd met several other guests throughout the day. Carl Tyrone and his girlfriend, Ann-Marie. Quinton Cullum, quarterback for Cavalier City High School, and his best friend, Don Blevins, who'd damaged his knee during the state play-offs. Don hobbled up and down the beach on crutches, staying pretty much to himself while the others swam and picnicked.

"Let's leave a note at the desk," Judy suggested. "Terry won't mind if he knows where to find you."

Reluctantly, he agreed, and they set off for the pier, hand in hand. He hadn't seen his parents since breakfast and wondered what they'd found to occupy their time. His dad, no doubt, was on the golf course, trying his best to outdo Judy's dad. Perry

Elton's competitive spirit never took a vacation.

"There you guys are." Ann-Marie McAnally glanced up from the paperback she was reading and adjusted her dark glasses to block out the sun. "Hasn't your friend shown up yet?" Carl, her boyfriend, was asleep on the blanket beside her.

"Not yet." Judy slipped out of her robe, draped it over her straw tote bag on the quilt she shared with Peter. "We decided to wait here."

Don Blevins stood near the water's edge, braced on one crutch, his leering gaze fixed on Judy's yellow bikini.

"Ignore him." Ann-Marie smiled up at Peter, round face and pudgy cheeks red from the sun. "He's too bashful to do anything but look."

"How do you know?" Judy asked.

"I talked to him while you were gone. Carl didn't like it, but I went over and introduced myself. I figure . . ." She stretched out again, on her stomach, and prepared to delve back into her novel. "If we're going to spend the summer together we should get to know each other. Don's definitely the shy type."

Shy or not, Peter wasn't sure he liked anyone ogling his girlfriend so blatantly. He was used to guys looking. Most of the time he felt honored that Judy had chosen him to go steady with. But there was something about the injured football player's brazenness that said he planned to do more than just enjoy Judy's beauty from a distance.

"Let's go for a swim." Judy slipped her arm through Peter's. "Maybe Terry will be here when we get back."

His best friend's arrival, as he waded into the

warm waters of Lake Sinter, was suddenly the least of his worries.

Bob Colby parked near the clubhouse at a quarter past six. Peter and Judy were on the porch again, along with Carl and Ann-Marie. Peter sat on the rail near the east end, swinging his legs from side to side, anxious to see what kind of mood Terry would be in when he stepped out of the van.

LuLu exited first. If she saw Peter, she ignored him, and chose instead to study her new surroundings with disdainful interest. She carried the baggy brown sweater she sometimes wore to school. In her left hand, she clutched her brown Bible.

Terry was the last one out, right after the Reverend and Mrs. Anderson.

"Hey, buddy." Peter bounded down the porch steps, rounding the fishpond in a few quick strides. "I thought you'd changed your mind or something."

"Nah." Terry glanced at his dad. "We took a side trip around the other side of Wild Horse Mountain. Lucinda's dad wanted to see Camp Hudgens."

"I'm glad you're here." Judy greeted him with a hug, surprising Terry as much as Peter. "Just wait until you meet some of the other kids. You're going to be glad you came." She led him toward the porch where Ann-Marie and Carl waited on a iron glider.

Terry glanced over his shoulder. LuLu stood alone, the sun mirrored in her thick lenses so that it was difficult to tell who she was looking at.

"Hey, Lucinda. Over here."

She crossed the lawn, head ducked, Bible and sweater clutched to her side.

"This is Judy Wand," Terry introduced them. "Peter's girlfriend."

LuLu nodded, a quick jerk of her chin, not the least bit friendly.

Judy stuck her hand out. "I've been looking forward to meeting you."

"You have?" She shook hands, glanced up for only a second. "Terry told me you'd be here. I . . ." She noticed Judy's short robe and bare feet and dropped her gaze again. Her cheeks were flushed, whether from embarrassment or disapproval Peter couldn't tell. "If you'll excuse me, I'd better join my parents. They wouldn't want me to wander off."

"You'll have to excuse Lucinda," Terry said when they were alone. "She's—"

"Weird," Peter said. "I told you." He watched as she stood beside her mother, her tan skirt so long the hem almost dragged on the ground.

"It's not her fault." Terry looked around, made sure they couldn't be overheard. "Her parents are really strict. Especially her old man."

"Peter said you'd probably get a sermon on the way here."

"Lucinda reads the Bible. So what? That doesn't make her a bad person."

Peter could only stare in disbelief. Terry was defending LuLu Anderson? He had been brainwashed somewhere between Scarletville and Sinter's Cove.

"I want you to meet Ann-Marie and Carl." Judy ended the awkward silence when they reached the first step. "They go to St. Edwards, in Albertville. Both of them will be seniors in the fall."

Terry was relaxed, more like his old self, by the time the introductions were made and he found out that Carl ran track for the St. Edwards team.

"I recognize you from the Bledsoe County meet last year." Carl was dark complected, several inches taller than Terry, and much more muscular. "You blew everyone away. I've never seen anyone run as fast as you did."

"Yeah." Terry tried to appear modest. "I was lucky."

"Our castle awaits." Bob Colby exited from the clubhouse lobby, followed close behind by Reverend Anderson. "Let's go, Virginia. Happy Hour started fifteen minutes ago."

"I've always wondered, Bob." LuLu's dad slipped his arm around the other man's shoulders. "Why do they call it Happy Hour?"

"Beats me. But if you'll meet me in the bar we can find out together."

No one expected the preacher to laugh, Peter least of all.

"If you're buying, friend." He slapped Bob Colby on the back. "I'll be there."

"I gotta go," Terry said as his group made their way toward the van. "I'll see you all later."

"Need some help unloading . . . ?"

He waved away Peter's offer. "Dad and I can handle the luggage, no problem." He waited beside the sliding door until the adults climbed on board. When it was LuLu's turn, he offered his hand and steadied her balance.

"Thank you." She smiled.

"You're welcome." He grinned, too, the way Peter did when he looked at Judy.

Peter wasn't sure if he wanted to laugh or cry. His best friend was, as his mother would say, smitten. But of all the girls to fall for, why LuLu Anderson?

"I'm telling you, Peter. Butt out. It's nobody's business but Terry's." Judy was always outspoken, but she usually tempered her comments if they were on opposing sides. "He could do worse. Lucinda seems . . . nice." She shook her head. "Okay, maybe nice isn't the right word. But it's obvious Terry sees some quality the rest of us have missed so far."

"Yeah? Like what? I'm telling you, she's got Terry brainwashed. He said it would happen, and . . ."

Judy paused in the middle of the trail that led from her cabin to the clubhouse. "Please. Let's not talk about them anymore until after dinner. It's our first evening together as a group and I didn't get all dressed up to talk about Terry's love life."

Peter exhaled, the debate ended. He noticed again, as he had when Judy had first greeted him at the door a few minutes ago, how beautiful she looked in her white dress, long hair spread over her shoulders, skin still pink from the hours she'd spent tanning on the beach. Her hemline was well above her knees. Don Blevins would probably fall off his crutches once he got a look at her legs tonight!

He slipped his arm around her waist and walked with her up the dusky trail where his mom, dad, and the others were waiting in the bar.

"If I know Terry, he'll be in and out of love a dozen times this summer."

Peter didn't reply. The fantasies he'd had ever since his parents announced the trip to Sinter's Cove were on the realm of reality. Moonlit strolls with Judy. Kisses beneath a starry sky. Terry was once again shoved to the back of his mind. He had other, more important things to think about.

"Besides." Judy squeezed his fingers. "If I didn't know better, I'd say you were jealous."

"Jealous?" He was ready to pick up the conversation in spite of his promises to concentrate on Judy, and only Judy, for the rest of the evening. "I'm not—"

"You and Terry had big plans for the summer. It's only natural for you to feel a little threatened now that Lucinda's in the picture."

"I don't feel . . ." He didn't have time to defend himself before they climbed to the top of the steps where a doorman, this one even older than the first, held the brass knob. He bowed as Judy swept past into the clubhouse lobby.

Bob Colby was well on his way to drunk by the time the maitre d' escorted the three families into the crowded dining room half an hour later. But no one seemed to notice, or care—least of all Reverend Anderson.

Most of the other tables and leather banquettes were occupied. Quinton Cullum, who sat alone with his parents, spoke as Peter and Judy passed by. There were two tables reserved, one for the adults, another for their children. Judy sat with her back to the window, LuLu on one side, and Peter on the other. Terry barely had time to get settled in his chair before Ann-Marie hurried over from where she was seated with her parents and Carl's mom and dad.

She was dressed in a black skirt and sweater, her neck and shoulders as sunburned as Judy's. "Hi, guys. There's going to be a party later at the pier, where we were today. Some girl from Elmore County is celebrating her birthday. I haven't met her yet. But her friend—Samantha Owensby—invited Carl and me. She told us to bring as many friends as we wanted. The more, the merrier."

"What time?" LuLu asked. "Will there be dancing? I want to wear comfortable shoes if there's going to be music."

Peter dropped his napkin on the floor. Obviously he wasn't the only one surprised. Terry's mouth was open wide enough to catch a baseball.

"Your mom and dad'll let you go?" he asked.

"As long as I adhere to their strict code of decorum, why shouldn't they? 'I will behave myself wisely in a perfect way.' Psalm 101."

"Excellent." Ann-Marie didn't seem the least bit fazed by LuLu's scripture-quoting. "We'll see you all at nine o'clock."

Peter ate his salad and tried not to let his disappointment show. He'd hoped to spend the evening alone with Judy, down by the beach. He should have known it wouldn't be easy to escape a crowd, especially since there were so many kids vacationing at Sinter's Cove this year.

An hour later, after their dishes were cleared away and dessert was served, the restaurant personnel sang "Happy Birthday" at a table near the entrance. Peter, like the others, strained to see the girl whose party they would attend later. The dining hall was filled to capacity, the waiters and chefs circled around the table, blocking his view. He could see only red helium-filled balloons tied to three chairs.

"Just think," Judy said as she leaned over and

rested her head on Peter's shoulder. "That'll be us in a few weeks."

"You have a birthday coming up?" LuLu folded her napkin beside her water glass. It was the first time she'd spoken to anyone except Terry since she'd accepted Ann-Marie's invitation. "Me, too. July 21st. I'll be eighteen."

"I'm older." Judy smiled. "I turn eighteen on July 7th."

"Peter and I were born the same day." Terry had been extraordinarily quiet, too, most of his attention focused on LuLu. He'd attempted to include her in conversations with Peter and Judy, but when she failed to cooperate, he scooted his chair nearer hers and the two of them spoke in hushed tones throughout the meal. "July 15th," he said.

Fifteen minutes later Peter waited in the lobby while Judy, LuLu, and Ann-Marie were in the ladies' room and Terry was outside, on the porch, with his mom and dad.

"Don't forget your curfew," Perry Elton said.

"Don't be silly, dear." His mother lingered outside the gift shop where she studied displays through plate glass windows. "It's vacation. Shouldn't Peter be allowed an extra hour, at least?"

"You're much too lenient, Margaret."

"But it's nearly nine o'clock now. By the time he changes into his casual clothes and meets the others, it will be well past." She wore a knitted shawl over a pink silk dress, and diamond earrings. "Besides . . ." She fluttered her eyelashes, something she knew irritated her husband. "I doubt *we'll* be home before midnight. You know how

you are when you play bridge. You won't quit until—''

"One minute past midnight and you're grounded
for the rest of the summer." He strolled off toward
the desk to leave a wake-up call for seven o'clock.

Peter was surprised his dad had given in so easily. "Thank you, Mother."

She kissed his cheek and hurried away without
a word.

His mother was right; it was close to nine-thirty
by the time he slipped into a pair of jeans and a T-
shirt and met Judy outside cabin 4.

"I'm sorry I ever doubted you, Peter." She held
his arm and walked beside him down a grassy slope
toward the pier. "This place is really wonderful
and I've had such a good time already. It was nice
of our parents to bring us here."

"I get to stay out till midnight." Freedom was
such a rare treat, he felt like celebrating.

"I thought you were still grounded for failing
Latin."

"All but forgotten . . ."

"My name's Samantha Owensby." She greeted
them the moment they arrived, a short girl with
pudgy cheeks like Ann-Marie, and dark blond hair
she wore in a braid down her back. Her voice was
surprisingly gruff for a girl so petite. "Ann-Marie
and Carl are over . . ." She had to tiptoe to see over
the shoulders of kids gathered near the bonfire.
"They were by the ice chests the last I saw them.
There's plenty to drink, so help yourself."

"Excuse me." Judy grabbed her before she had
a chance to escape. "We haven't met the girl
whose birthday we're celebrating. Think you can
point her out?"

"You can't miss Becca. She's the only girl here whose nose is pierced. Her parents let her do it last week as an early present."

"This should be interesting," Peter mumbled as they made their way through the crowd.

Someone turned on a stereo, full blast, and music echoed across Lake Andrew Sinter. Judy excused herself a minute later, as soon as they met up with Ann-Marie, and the two of them went off to find the girl with the ring in her nose. Peter hung back, near the fringe of revelers, and looked for Terry, the only other guy he knew who hated a crowd of strangers as much as he did. He recognized most of the kids from the restaurant, but a few of them must have eaten in their cabins. The mob grew larger by the minute. Before long he found himself standing shoulder to shoulder with Don Blevins.

"Some party, huh?" Peter remarked casually.

Don shrugged, turned his head the other way.

Peter—tempted to kick the boy's crutches out from under him—walked away instead and found Judy a few minutes later, deep in conversation with a group of girls, including Ann-Marie, LuLu, and the guest of honor. What Becca wore in her nose was not anything as simple as what Peter had expected. Atop a small gold hoop was a silver butterfly no larger than a pencil eraser. He tried not to stare, and probably would have asked her if it hurt, if Judy hadn't stopped him with her elbow.

Several guys loitered nearby, at the top of a sandy knoll, too busy girl-watching to make idle chatter. One of them, a kid with long hair and a Grateful Dead T-shirt, had definitely zeroed-in on Judy.

"Becca, this is my boyfriend." She squeezed his

hand, a silent message that she'd missed him. "Peter, meet Rebecca King."

"My friends call me Becca." She was, in spite of her short flame-red and black hair, and butterfly in her nose, one of the prettiest girls on the beach.

Now this, Peter thought, was the kind of girl Terry needed to fall for.

"Nice to meet you."

"If you're looking for Terry . . ." LuLu pushed her hair behind her ear, the flames of the bonfire reflected in her thick lenses. "He went to get us something to drink. But that was a while ago. I expected him back before now."

"I'll see if I can find him. If you'll excuse me, ladies."

"He's cute," he heard Becca say as he shoved his way through the crowd to the ice chests and refreshments. He grabbed a cola and spied Terry sitting in the shadows, well away from the mob.

"Hey, buddy. What're you doing up here?"

"Killing time." He swayed to the music, not in the mood to talk.

"Everything okay?" Peter sat on the ground beside him and popped the ring on his soft drink.

Terry gulped his Coke and belched. "Now that you mention it, no."

"What's going on?"

"Something weird."

"You mean . . . you and LuLu?" Peter took a sip and prepared himself for an in-depth conversation. He'd wondered how long it would be before his best friend realized that his infatuation was the result of being cooped up with the Andersons most of the day. He should have known Terry would come around as soon as he'd gotten a good look at some of the girls here tonight.

"I didn't mean Lucinda." His voice was oddly distant. Peter recognized the warning signals right away. Terry was defensive, the way he had been before they left Scarletville. "It's this place that's weird, man."

"You're not having a good time?"

"Maybe it's my imagination. But—"

"But what?" Peter asked.

"Tonight at dinner, when I looked around the restaurant, I thought it was strange that . . ." Terry shifted his weight, readjusted his ball cap so the bill was pulled over his eyes. Whatever was on his mind had him troubled. And he wasn't prepared to share his suspicions yet. Not even with his best friend.

Peter took another long swallow and fought back his impatience. Why couldn't Terry trust him, quit beating around the bush? Hadn't they always been able to tell each other anything, no matter how strange it might sound to the other?

"How many kids would you guess are staying at the Cove this summer?" Terry asked.

"I don't know. Most of them are here tonight. Thirty-five. Forty."

"How many have you met so far?"

He counted quickly to himself. Ann-Marie, Carl, Samantha, Rebecca, Quinton, and his friend, Don Blevins, the jerk.

"Half a dozen. Why?"

"What's the one thing they have in common?"

He could think of a lot of possibilities offhand, but he wasn't sure his answers were what Terry wanted to hear.

"What do we have in common?"

"Our birthdays."

"What else?"

"We live in Scarletville."

"And?"

"I don't know, Ter. You're giving me a headache with all these questions."

Terry crushed his empty pop can and rose to his feet. He was gone before Peter could stop him, but not far—at the edge of the crowd where Carl Tyrone was talking to the long-haired kid in the Grateful Dead T-shirt.

"I want to ask you guys something," Terry said when Peter finally caught up.

"Shoot," Carl said.

"You have any brothers?"

"No."

"Sisters?"

"Nope."

"What about you?"

The guy in the T-shirt looked at Terry, eyes narrowed suspiciously. He looked wiry enough to fight anyone on the beach and come out on the winning end. "Who wants to know?"

"It's not important." Peter grabbed the back of Terry's windbreaker and led him in the direction where he'd last seen Judy and the others. "So Carl's an only child, and maybe the other guy too. Why's that such a big deal?"

LuLu's sudden appearance ended their discussion. "I have to leave now, Terry. It's ten minutes till curfew."

"Would you . . ." He lowered his voice, hoping Peter wouldn't hear. "Like me to walk you to your cabin?"

66

"That would be nice. Thank you."

Judy came to his side the instant they were gone. "Where've you been? Not giving Terry a hard time about Lucinda, I hope."

"Nah." He'd intended to, but the conversation had taken a wild turn. "He has some crazy notion—"

Music blared from the speakers, drowned out his voice. Samantha Owensby, in faded jeans and blue sweatshirt, wove her way past the bonfire, so short Peter caught only a glimpse of her blond braid now and again.

She was almost on the other side before she spied Judy and rushed over. "Have you seen Becca? It's time to sing 'Happy Birthday,' but I can't find her anywhere."

"I'll help you look." Judy walked away, returned a second later. "Don't go anywhere, Peter. We've hardly spent any time together since we got here. I won't be gone a minute."

"Yeah." He nodded. "It shouldn't be hard to find Becca. She sticks out like a sore thumb."

She giggled, kissed him on the cheek. "Be nice. Becca thinks you're cute."

He didn't see Judy again until a few minutes before midnight.

He never saw Rebecca King again.

Six

"Wake up, sleepyhead."

Peter opened his eyes. Morning light streamed through the open curtains and he knew instinctively that he'd slept past the time his dad usually roused him from bed.

"What time is it?"

His mom picked his jeans and shirt from the floor and folded them on top of the dresser. "Ten-thirty. Judy's waiting for you in the kitchen."

"Where's Father?" Wherever he was, one thing was for certain. He'd be upset because Peter had overslept and missed breakfast.

"He left first thing with Bob Colby and Reverend Anderson. I'd guess they're about to wind up a round by golf by now."

Peter threw back the covers, grabbed his jeans and a clean shirt from the top drawer, and hurried into his bathroom to strip off his pajamas. After a quick shower, he ran downstairs while he combed his hair with his fingers, and found Judy at the table with his mother.

She looked up, tried to smile, and he knew instantly that something was wrong.

"If you'll excuse me." His mother drained the

remainder of her coffee in the sink. "I never did finish unpacking yesterday." She patted Judy's shoulder as she left the room.

"Some vacation. I spend all my time sleeping." Peter poured himself a glass of orange juice from the small refrigerator and joined Judy at the table a moment later. There was a full tumbler, untouched, in front of her.

"Becca's gone," she said. "Checked out. The desk clerk said Mr. King turned in their cabin key late last night. Probably about the time we were looking for her on the beach."

"Why?" Peter felt lethargic, not yet fully awake. He rubbed his swollen eyes and tried to concentrate on what Judy was telling him. There had to be an explanation, something that made sense. "What's Samantha say?"

"She's more shocked than anyone. She's Becca's best friend, after all." Judy reached for her glass, changed her mind, and leaned back in her rattan chair. She moved as slow as Peter, though for different reasons. It was obvious from the circles under her eyes that she hadn't slept well the night before.

"What can I do?" Peter asked.

"Talk to the desk clerk." Judy answered so quickly he knew she'd anticipated his question and planned her strategy in advance. "She won't tell Samantha much. She hardly even answered our questions. Maybe if you talk to her . . ."

He forgot about breakfast, told his mom he was leaving, and met Judy on the porch. The day was hot; long shadows stretched across the path as they walked toward the clubhouse and registration desk.

"Have you seen Terry this morning?" Peter asked.

Judy nodded, her thoughts somewhere far away. "He and Lucinda were waiting for the gift shop to open. I don't know where they went after that."

He climbed the porch steps, nodding to the doorman on his way to the lobby. Judy remained out of sight. It was part of her plan, she said. Maybe the clerk wouldn't be so hesitant to answer questions if she thought Peter was just another friend wondering why Becca had left the resort so unexpectedly.

The conversation lasted five minutes and provided less information than Judy or Samantha had learned earlier. The woman behind the desk, in a white linen jacket, a gold scarf tied around her neck, had not been on duty when Mr. King had handed in the key to cabin 6. She hadn't been told their reasons for leaving. Perhaps it was a medical emergency . . . or something to do with Becca's parents' jobs . . . maybe a death in the family. The possibilities, Peter knew, were limitless.

Judy talked to the doorman while Peter was inside. Since there was no one in that position from eleven at night till seven in the morning, he didn't even know the Kings had checked out, much less why.

"Let's find Samantha," Judy suggested. "Maybe's she heard something by now."

They went by her cabin first, but no one answered the door, so they checked the one place they were most likely to find her: the beach. Samantha was on a blanket with Ann-Marie. Carl, asleep on an inflatable raft, floated a short distance from the water's edge. There were other kids on the bank, most of them stretched out in the sun, hoping to return home with the perfect tan.

"Mom says I shouldn't worry. I'll probably hear from Becca as soon as she's able to contact me." Samantha, though still concerned, seemed determined not to let her friend's hasty exit ruin the rest of her vacation. "I wanted to call, but Mom said no long distance charges. I'm still in trouble from February, when I was at the skating rink and I met this guy who lived out of town. I called him every day for two weeks . . ."

Peter wandered off in search of Terry. As much as he wanted to be with Judy, he didn't want to be around her new friends once they started to discuss guys. He'd catch up with her later; maybe they could have lunch together.

He found Terry and LuLu on the pier, Terry in his swimming trunks, baseball cap and sneakers. The preacher's daughter was in the same skirt and blouse she'd worn yesterday. Only her brown sweater was missing.

Terry waved as soon as he saw Peter. LuLu never acknowledged his presence. Not even after he strode down the weathered planks and sat beside Terry.

"I came by," Terry said. "Your old man said you were asleep."

"You should have woke me."

"I will. Next time."

LuLu stood after a few minutes of silence and grabbed her Bible. "Mama expects me to help with lunch. I'll see you later, Terry."

"She doesn't like me," Peter said when she was gone.

Terry shook his head. "No."

71

"She thinks I'm a bad influence on you."

He spat in the lake. "She's right."

Neither of them mentioned LuLu again. Judy found them twenty minutes later, still on the pier, and suggested they join some of the others—Carl, Ann-Marie, and Quinton Cullum—in the coffee shop for burgers and fries. Peter jumped to his feet, eager to go. Since Becca's disappearance no longer seemed as dire as it had that morning, his appetite was back, full-force. He was disappointed when Terry declined the invitation, saying he had plans of his own.

"What plans?" Peter insisted.

Terry tugged on his cap, shielded his eyes from the sun. "Nothing important."

"They can wait then."

"Nah. You guys go ahead. I'll catch up with you later."

"He'll still be there, waiting, when LuLu comes back," Peter mumbled, looked at Judy, and expected her to comment on his jealous tirade. She remained quiet all the way to the restaurant.

He didn't see his best friend again until four o'clock that afternoon. Peter was dozing on Judy's quilt, the sun beating down on his shoulders. He knew he should roll over—he was hot, sweaty, his flesh no doubt burned—but he was just too tired and lazy.

Terry nudged Peter's arm with his sneaker. "You asleep?"

"Not anymore, I'm not." He turned on his side, reached for his sunglasses. "Where've you been?"

"Looking around. There's a cove about half a mile up the bank, on the other side of those rocks."

He pointed north, beyond the soggy ashes from last night's bonfire. "You interested?"

"Sure." He started to rise.

Terry motioned him to lie still. "Not now. Tonight. Can you meet me around ten?"

"I . . ." He hated to admit it, but since he'd gained an hour on his curfew last night, he'd probably lose one today. "I'll ask Dad and let you know."

"Maybe you shouldn't. Tell your old man, that is."

"He's not going to let me out of his sight unless he knows where I'm going."

"Don't mention the cove. Just tell him we—"

"Do you know what'll happen if I'm caught lying? I'll get grounded for the rest of the summer."

Terry knelt on the bank, hands between his knees, and didn't respond right away. "I wasn't going to tell you until later. After I had time to think about it."

"Think about what?" Peter asked.

"I wanted to make sure I didn't jump to conclusions, let my imagination run wild the way I did last night."

Peter sat up, toweled the sweat off his shoulders. "What're you talking about? Not that crap about—"

"No." Terry shook his head. If he was insulted, his expression didn't show. "This is different."

He opened his right fist. Cradled in his palm was a gold hoop and silver butterfly.

"I found this about an hour after you and Judy went to lunch. Tangled up in some grass and dead cattails in the cove."

"It's Becca's?"

"Probably." Terry closed his fist, securing the nose ring out of sight. "But why'd she leave without it? I thought we'd go back, look around . . ."

Judy appeared behind Terry, her long hair plastered to her face and shoulders, yellow bikini dripping water.

"What're you guys talking about? I thought I heard you mention Becca's name."

Peter smiled, handed her his towel. "Didn't you tell me last night that she never took off her nose ring?"

"She's only had it a short time, but she never went anywhere without it. Samantha said Mr. King hated it so much, Becca wore it just to irritate him. Plus, once she put it on, she felt naked without it. So she wore it all the time." She dried her hair, satisfied his questions had been answered, and reached for her tote bag. "Guess what. Ann-Marie told me Carl's birthday is day after tomorrow. I thought it would be fun to give him a surprise party." She dragged a comb through her tangled hair. "What do you guys think? I don't want to do anything that will make Samantha feel bad. But we can't not have any more parties just because her best friend's gone."

Peter tried to relax, to concentrate on the plans Judy mapped out for Carl Tyrone's birthday. But his thoughts returned to the ring every few seconds. There had to be an explanation. The hoop and butterfly, though exactly like the one Rebecca wore in her nose, was probably sold in a lot of stores and could have been lost weeks before, by someone they'd never met. What were the odds that the one Terry had found belonged to Becca? Especially since the cove was hard to get to and Becca had

74

had no reason to go there. Samantha would know, but it was probably best to keep quiet for now. He didn't want to ask any more stupid questions that would make him look like a fool in Judy's eyes. And that's exactly what she'd call him if she knew he were about to risk his vacation on little more than a hunch.

Hopefully, once he and Terry returned to the cove, they'd find something to prove Becca had never been there. Her departure was sudden, even suspicious, but there was no sense in involving anyone else if they didn't have to.

"Are you bored?"

"Of course not." Peter slipped his arm around Judy's shoulders and, with the heels of his shoes, sent the porch swing swaying back and forth.

Peter glanced at his watch again. Ten minutes till ten. And he still hadn't thought of a way to meet Terry without arousing his dad's or Judy's suspicions.

"That's the third time you've looked at your watch in the last five minutes." Judy moved to the edge of the swing, out of his reach. "If I didn't know better, I'd say you were anxious to get rid of me."

"Of course not," he said again.

"It doesn't matter." Judy stood, grabbed her jacket from a wicker chair beside the door. "I told Mom I wouldn't stay out late. Can you walk me home?"

Bless you, Judy, he said to himself as he went in to ask his dad's permission. Judy had come through for him again, even if she didn't know it.

Perry Elton folded the sports section in his lap.

"Do you have your key? Margaret and I will probably be in bed by the time you get back."

"Yes, sir. I'll try not to wake you."

Judy yawned once they were in the darkness, though she turned aside so Peter couldn't see.

"Now who's bored?" he asked.

"Not bored, Peter. Tired. I'll sleep better tonight knowing Becca's okay."

Mr. and Mrs. Wand were on the porch swing of cabin 4. Mr. Wand's head rested in his wife's lap as she massaged the silver hair at his temple. He sat up the moment he heard his daughter's footsteps.

"Hi, kids."

"Good evening, Mr. Wand," Peter said. "Mrs. Wand."

"Would you like to stay for a glass of tea?" Judy's mom made no effort to rise, so Peter declined the offer, saying his parents expected him back before too long.

He squeezed Judy's hand—he didn't dare kiss her good night in front of her parents—and returned to the shadows at the edge of the path they'd taken moments before. He hadn't counted on the Wands to be outside, to take note of what time he'd left their cabin to return to his own. Chances were slim, he knew, that the topic would come up the next day when they talked to his parents. Still, he was about to break one of his mom's and dad's rules, and if he got caught, the consequences wouldn't be pleasant.

He followed the trail toward cabin 17 until he was positive he was out of sight of Judy and her parents, then darted down a grassy slope to the picket fence. He didn't bother to open the gate. He

76

climbed over instead, and found Terry at the end of the pier a few minutes later.

"You're late."

"I'm lucky I'm here at all." He was as nervous as Terry. Both of them stood, hands in their hip pockets, and stared at the rocks that jutted above the lake half a mile away. "What is it we hope to find?" Peter asked.

"Beats me."

"Did you bring a flashlight?" Peter asked.

"I hoped you would." Terry zipped the front of his track jacket and strode toward the area where, twenty-four hours ago, they'd gotten together to celebrate Rebecca King's birthday.

The beach was deserted. Boating and swimming after dark were prohibited, unless the resort manager gave special permission. Peter wished he knew how often this section of the Cove was patrolled by security guards who strolled the grounds at night.

Terry was well past the bonfire by the time Peter caught up. "Tell me again, Ter, why are we going to so much trouble?"

"A girl leaves without so much as a word to anyone, even her best friend, because of a family emergency. I don't buy it."

Terry's reasons might sound without merit to most people, but not to Peter. If he had to cancel his vacation, no matter how much his parents rushed him, he'd never leave without saying good-bye to his friends. Of course he didn't know Rebecca all that well . . . she might not be so considerate. Still, if Terry hadn't found the nose ring in the opposite direction from where she was

77

last seen, he might have accepted her departure with fewer questions of his own.

Peter shivered, wished he'd thought to grab a jacket before he walked Judy home. Evenings were chilly at Sinter's Cove, especially this near the lake. He glanced at his watch. Ten-fifteen. He had only a few minutes—another quarter-hour at the most—before his parents started to wonder where he was, if they weren't already asleep.

Terry was accustomed to running long distances. But Peter wasn't. He had to stop and catch his breath the moment they reached the crag. Up close, the incline was steeper than he had suspected. Climbing to the other side would be treacherous. Especially in such dim light.

Terry scaled the first ten yards, stomach pressed against a boulder for support, and swung his right foot onto the next ledge.

"There's plenty of toeholds if you can find them in the dark," he said. He glanced over his shoulder, face hidden in shadows. "If you slip, try to land in the water. You're less likely to hurt yourself that way."

Peter groaned, watched as his best friend continued to clamber up and over the rocks as agile as a mountain goat. Terry was halfway to the other side. Peter was only a few inches off the ground; he could have changed his mind and jumped down without so much as a twisted ankle.

"Are you coming, or what?" Terry's voice was muffled, distant.

Peter found that his sneakers were perfect for climbing, the soles sturdy enough to give him a firm grip and enough confidence not to lag so far behind.

Terry, arms splayed out on either side, waited at the most dangerous point, where the rocks sloped toward Lake Andrew Sinter at a near-ninety degree angle and there were fewer places to grab hold.

Peter looked down, saw only a few lights reflected in the water, and forced himself to concentrate on what lay on the other side. Solid ground. He'd lost sight of why they'd risked injury—remembered Rebecca King—and decided her reasons for leaving were no longer important. The challenge was to reach the cove safely. And get back, of course, before his parents found out he'd let Terry talk him into coming here in the first place.

He approached the other side, slipped once near the bottom, and managed to join his best friend on the muddy bank with only a scraped elbow.

"Where'd you find the butterfly?" Now that he was here, there was no time to waste.

Terry moved through the shadows, onto a rock slick with moss. "It's so darn dark . . . The cattails are here somewhere. There's a big pile, too many to walk around. I stepped over them this afternoon and just happen to glance down. That when I found Becca's ring."

Peter didn't think it important to remind him that they had no proof it was hers, and, because they'd come here at night when it was impossible to see, they would probably return empty-handed. Rebecca King was probably safe. There was nothing here to say otherwise. She might even be showing off her recently pierced nose for another group of strangers at this very minute.

Peter walked a few steps, not yet across the moss-covered rock, when he heard a voice he was positive didn't belong to Terry.

Terry froze, one foot in the air like a bird dog tracking its prey. "Did you hear that?"

"Forgive us our trespasses . . ."

The voice, vaguely familiar, though Peter still couldn't identify its owner, echoed through the narrow canyon.

"As we forgive those who trespass against us."

Only one person would recite the Lord's Prayer this time of night, in such a remote area.

"LuLu? What the heck are you doing here?" Terry, too stunned to be polite, called her by the nickname she hated.

Peter moved forward until he had a clear view of the preacher's daughter, on her knees beside the pile of cattails. Head bowed, eyes closed. The wind gusted through the pages of her Bible.

"Lead us not into temptation . . ."

Terry backed against the cliff, out of sight.

"Deliver us from evil . . ." She rose a moment later, after a heartfelt Amen! and saw only Peter in the moonlight. "How dare you follow me."

"I didn't." He realized why he disliked LuLu. She made him feel guilty even when he hadn't done anything wrong. "How'd you get here?"

"I took the same path as you, I imagine." She hugged herself, turned sideways so the slight breeze swept limp hair out of her eyes. "What, may I ask, are you doing?"

"I . . ." Peter stammered, not sure what to tell her. "We . . ." Terry was the one who had a crush on her; let him explain.

His best friend moved into the light, toward the cattails. "We didn't expect to find you. We didn't expect to find anyone."

Lucinda's anger faded when she realized that Peter wasn't alone. "You," she said, smiling, "are the last person I thought I'd see tonight."

"You climbed the cliff?" Terry glanced at her long skirt and brown leather shoes. "You could have hurt yourself."

"The Lord is my shepherd. He leadeth me beside the still waters. I came here last night during the party to pray. And I returned tonight. It's very peaceful."

"You can't pray in your room where it's safe?" Peter asked.

LuLu disapproved of him so much, that no matter what he said, it was wrong. "I can talk to God wherever I am. Something you might try once in a while."

Her holier-than-thou attitude was a real pain in the neck. If he wanted a sermon, he'd go to church . . . and started to tell her that before Terry interrupted.

"You were here last night?"

She nodded. "I had just returned to the party when you asked if you could walk me home."

"Did you see anyone, talk to anybody?"

"No." She grabbed her Bible from the ground, placed it protectively beneath her sweater, and walked around Peter to begin her ascent to the other side. "I have to leave. If Papa finds me, he'll think I came here to meet you."

"We'll go, too." Terry was so wrapped up in LuLu's presence, he'd forgotten their reasons for coming to the cove. "I can't let you climb the cliffs alone."

"I'm capable of taking care of myself." She scaled the first ledge, skirt billowed around her an-

81

kles, Bible tucked in her elastic waistband. "But thank you, Terry, for your concern."

Peter wasn't going to let her escape that easily. He'd risked a lot to find out what he could about Rebecca and had come up empty-handed. LuLu might know something that would help put his mind at ease.

"Are you sure you didn't see anyone last night?"

She ignored him and climbed up another few feet.

"The girl whose birthday we celebrated last night," Terry said. "She didn't happen to be here, did she?"

LuLu paused, her hip pressed against a giant boulder. "I heard someone. I can't say for sure, but I thought I recognized her voice. She was upset and I thought she used language I could never repeat."

Rebecca was here. And not by herself. "Who was she talking to?" Peter asked.

LuLu started not to answer, but decided she would, if only for Terry's benefit.

"I hid when I realized I wasn't alone. I thought it was a couple who'd come here to . . ." She ducked her head, embarrassed. "I didn't want to be accused of spying."

"But you overheard their conversation?" Terry asked.

"No. I was near the bank, on the other side of those cattails. The wind was blowing. The waves weren't as calm as they are tonight. I couldn't really hear a word. I really must go before Papa comes looking for me."

It was past time for Peter to leave, too. He'd

have a lot of explaining to do if his mom and dad had waited up. Terry scaled the terrain as quickly as before, until he was only an arm's length behind Lucinda.

Peter moved at a slower pace, purposely lagging behind. Terry was his friend—and though Peter might not approve—he deserved a few minutes alone with LuLu before they reached the beach and had to say good night.

The questions that had brought them here had been answered in part. But not enough that they knew any more than when they had first climbed over the cliffs. Becca was definitely in the cove last night. Odds were the ring belonged to her. She'd left it behind, whether by accident or on purpose Peter didn't know, and gone off with her parents without a word to anyone. Or so he'd thought until a few minutes ago. Becca had been upset with someone. LuLu had witnessed the confrontation. What the conversation was about, and who it was with, was still anybody's guess.

Peter knew without being told that he and Terry wouldn't talk again until morning. Since the Colbys' and Andersons' cabins were next door to each other, it was only natural he'd head in that direction with LuLu and leave Peter to make his own way home.

A half hour had passed. Peter checked his watch twice (the numbers were so difficult to see in the dark), and decided he'd tell Judy first thing tomorrow what he'd done. She'd probably be disappointed he hadn't shared his plans earlier, angry because he didn't ask her to come along. Maybe he'd ask his dad for an advance on his allowance so he could rent a canoe. He and Judy would find a secluded spot, share a picnic lunch, and spend the rest of the afternoon alone. That, after all, was the reason he'd looked forward to Sinter's Cove.

He approached the wind-scattered ashes of the bonfire, the pier just ahead, when he saw someone standing near the water's edge. The weathered pilings were bathed in white, the lake as dark as ink. He slowed up, stopped walking altogether when he recognized Judy's voice. And realized she wasn't alone.

She was barefoot, jeans rolled above her ankles, white blouse open at the collar. Her long hair, tied with a ribbon, blew across her back.

Beside her was Don Blevins, his weight resting on crutches.

SEVEN

Tuesday passed. Judy never mentioned her rendez-vous with Don. Wednesday she was too busy with final arrangements for Carl's party to spend much time with Peter.

He was in a lousy mood.

"What's eating you?" Terry stood at the edge of the Eltons' porch as Peter pushed himself back and forth in the swing. His mom and dad had gone off soon after five o'clock to meet the Colbys and Andersons for a cocktail before dinner. Judy had convinced the manager and head chef to sponsor a weiner roast in Carl's honor. Peter and Terry were supposed to meet him here at six o'clock and keep him occupied until it was time to spring the surprise.

"I said—"

"I heard you." Peter stopped the swing, sat with his shoulders against the hard slats, and wished the heck his mind would quit listing all kinds of reasons why Judy would be on the beach with Don Blevins. Late at night.

"Boy, are you in a bad mood," Terry said.

"Yeah, I am." He hadn't told anyone, not even his best friend, what he'd witnessed two nights ago.

He was too shaken up, too embarrassed. Judy was going to dump him for a creep like Blevins? Or maybe she didn't plan to break up with him . . . Maybe she planned to play him for a fool, meet Don every chance she got, and still have her steady boyfriend when she returned home at the end of the summer.

Some vacation this had turned out to be.

"Wanna talk about it?" Terry asked.

"Nah." He did, but didn't know how to start. Terry would tell him to put aside his injured pride and confront Judy, which was really the only sensible thing to do. Her reasons for walking on the beach with another guy might be innocent. Yeah. Right. And LuLu Anderson might be elected Homecoming Queen next year.

"Carl ought to be here any minute." Terry walked to the porch steps, adjusted his cap. "What'd we plan to do until time to go to the beach?"

"I hadn't thought about it," Peter answered.

"Well, hadn't you better? Judy gave you strict orders—"

"I'm gonna beat the crap out of Don Blevins."

"That'll take five minutes." He leaned against the wooden rail. "What're we gonna do the rest of the time?"

Peter didn't laugh, though Terry's flippant manner was exactly what he needed to draw him out of his current mood.

Carl arrived a few minutes later. "You guys are just about the ugliest baby-sitters I've ever had." He bounded onto the porch steps, leaned against the rail opposite Terry. "Ann-Marie says I'm not to go near the pier until after dark. Let's see, I wonder why. It wouldn't have anything to do with my birthday, would it?''

"Is today your birthday?" Terry was not a good liar, and even worse actor. "I had no idea. Congratulations.''

"Yeah. Right.'' Carl was, as Judy had described him, tall, dark, and handsome, with a perfect smile and the kind of devil-may-care attitude Peter admired. "What'd you say we go to the lobby and wait. Quinton Cullum told me there's a billiards table in the lounge. We could shoot a couple of rounds, a dollar a ball. If you're in the mood to lose your money.''

Carl talked more—filling them in on his school, his friends, and his involvement with the track team—than he had since his arrival Saturday. He spent most of his time with Ann-Marie, and who had a chance to talk with her around? he said. His parents had cancelled their original vacation plans, to visit relatives he'd never met in Canada and California, and opted to come along with the McAnallys when they'd extended an invitation to Sinter's Cove. He'd met Ann-Marie at a Little League ball game when he was twelve and had never been interested in another girl since. They wanted to marry this time next year, right after graduation, though neither of them had discussed their plans with their parents yet. The McAnallys would probably throw a fit; no guy would be good enough for their daughter unless he were a doctor or a lawyer. Carl worked part-time at a supermarket in the meat department.

Peter lost big time to the other two guys. Try as he might, he couldn't concentrate enough to line up his cue stick and make a decent shot. Though he refused to think about Judy, either. He was glad when he looked at his watch and it was time to escort Carl to the beach.

Carl stuffed the bills into his pocket, slapped Terry on the back on their way out the door, and thanked them both for a profitable evening. Terry didn't mind losing, since Carl was such a good sport, but Peter wondered how he'd make it till Friday without an advance on his allowance. After tonight, it might not matter. He and Judy could be history and he'd have no one to spend money on except himself.

Judy and the others had outdone themselves. Given more time for this party than Rebecca's, they'd strung paper lanterns at the top of the wooden pilings, set tables with white linen cloths borrowed from the kitchen staff, and arranged for more extravagant refreshments. Even the music, blasting from the same stereo as before, sounded better.

LuLu and Judy poured crushed ice and orange juice into a punch bowl as Peter approached the tables at the north end. The moon was bright, the sky laden with clouds. He could see the cliffs in the distance silhouetted behind LuLu's shoulders, the uppermost ridges lost in gray mist.

LuLu glanced up, spotted Peter, and went back to her task without acknowledging his presence. Judy greeted him with a kiss, accepted his congratulations for a job well done, and put him to work immediately. He removed plastic wrap from trays of hors d'oeuvres and bowls of chili, shredded cheese, and relish.

Carl pretended to be surprised, smiled modestly through three choruses of "For He's a Jolly Good

Fellow,'' and wandered off into the shadows to spend a few minutes alone with Ann-Marie.

Peter finished his assigned duty, asked Judy what else he could do, and searched the crowd for Don Blevins. The football player sat on a log near the fire, an ice chest open in front of him, as he handed packages of wieners to Quinton Cullum and the long-haired kid who'd worn a Grateful Dead T-shirt to Rebecca's party. Don was laughing, having a good time, and Peter was tempted to go over and smack him upside the head with one of his crutches. But, he couldn't very well challenge a guy who was recuperating from surgery, could he? That would lose Judy for sure.

"Something wrong?" Judy asked. "You look like you're upset."

He loved Judy. He realized that now more than before and wanted to do anything possible to make her forget about any other guy.

"Can we talk later? I need to ask you—"

"Sure." She wiped her hands on a paper towel. "But let me help Quinton and Don with the hot dogs first. I told 'em be careful and not burn 'em . . .''

He didn't talk to Judy again for an hour.

Terry and LuLu were on an army blanket with Ann-Marie, Styrofoam plates and paper napkins weighted down with cups of ice so they wouldn't blow away and litter the beach. Judy was at one end of the crowd with Quinton, a black plastic bag stretched between them, as they moved among the guests and gathered trash. She'd asked Peter to help do the same at the opposite side. He followed Samantha Owensby, as the girl with the blond braid chatted on and on.

"I don't care what Mom says, I'm going to call later tonight, even if I get in trouble."

"Sorry," he said when he realized Samantha expected a response. "What'd you say?"

"I still haven't heard from Becca. And I'm more than a little peeved. It was inconsiderate of her to leave without saying good-bye. How hard can it be to pick up a telephone and let me know she's okay?"

"Maybe she's grounded," Peter suggested. "Maybe she's not allowed to talk to her friends."

"Grounded? For what?"

"I don't know. I just thought maybe she'd done something she wasn't supposed to do and that's the reason her parents took her away."

"Mr. and Mrs. King are too lenient for that." Samantha shook her head, tugged on her side of the trash bag, and walked toward a gang of kids standing beneath the lanterns. "They let Becca get by with murder. Always have."

He knew few parents who would allow their daughter to dye her hair bright red, much less let her pierce her nose, and buy her a butterfly nose ring as a birthday present.

"Becca's in some kind of trouble. But not because she'd done anything wrong. I don't know why I didn't think of this before. I'll call collect. Becca's parents won't mind." She handed him her side of the trash bag and hurried up the grassy slope toward the cabins.

Ten minutes later he stuffed the bag into a barrel at the end of the refreshment table and went to find Judy. She was seated on the log, Quinton Cullum at one end, Don Blevins on the other.

"Hi." She motioned for him to sit beside her.

"I was wondering . . . can we take a walk?" It was time to face the facts, ask the questions that had been buzzing around in his head for two days. Besides, the last person he wanted to be around right now was Don.

Judy grabbed her glass of punch, slid her arm through Peter's, and walked with him past the pier.

"You're awfully serious. I hope you're not about to break up with me."

"I hope I'm not either," he said, quietly, so she couldn't hear.

LuLu stopped them before they had a chance to leave. "Ann-Marie wants to know when you plan to cut the cake. She's gone to look for Carl. But that's been ten minutes ago. I haven't seen her since."

"Tell her I'm with Peter. If she wants to start without me, that's okay."

There was something changed about LuLu tonight. Some small distinction he didn't notice until now. His thoughts were too preoccupied with Judy and the conversation ahead to give the preacher's daughter more than a passing glance.

"Did you notice how nice Lucinda looks?" Judy asked as they strolled toward the cliffs.

"Umm," he said. "Something's changed. I don't know what."

"She's wearing makeup, silly." Judy laughed, nudged him with her elbow. "I didn't expect you to notice. But Terry saw the change right away. She's actually very pretty, you know. I told her we'd go to the mall once we got back to Scarletville. She needs a new wardrobe that doesn't make her look so frumpy. And a haircut that—"

"I didn't come here to talk about LuLu."

91

"That's a terrible nickname," Judy said. "She hates it."

"I don't want to talk about Lucinda. I want to talk about . . ." Now that the moment was at hand, he didn't know how to start. No matter what he said—what questions he asked—he'd sound like a jealous boyfriend making accusations.

"You and Don," he said.

"Blevins?" She turned and looked at him. "What about us?"

"I saw you. I . . ." His throat was dry, his thoughts so jumbled and frantic that he had a difficult time putting them into words. "I wasn't spying on you or anything." Now he needed to explain why he'd been on the beach when he'd led her to believe he was headed home, too. "Terry and I went to the cove on the other side of those rocks. Lu . . . cinda was there, and—"

"I know. She told me all about it."

"She did? When?"

"Tonight. While we were getting dressed for the party."

"Then you know when I saw you with Don it was by accident." He felt a little calmer, though he still chose his words carefully. Prying into Judy's business and upsetting her wouldn't make the answers any easier to hear.

"I should have guessed that's why you've been so distant." She sounded relieved, not the least bit angry she'd been caught.

He exhaled, felt the tension drain from his body. Judy would have reacted differently if her motives had been as awful as he had imagined.

"I had something to discuss with Don. In private."

"What?"

"Please don't ask me, Peter. I can't tell you."
She leaned against his shoulder, tightened her grip
on his arm. "If you're thinking it was some kind
of romantic tryst, you're wrong. Don's a nice guy.
He would never—"

"Yeah. Right." He left any further comments
unspoken. Now was the perfect time to prove how
much he trusted Judy. He might have recognized
the leer in Don's eyes, might not believe his intentions were so innocent, but that wasn't Judy's fault.

He felt better. A little.

"If I tell you it's something you'll find out eventually, will you promise not to let it bother you so
much?"

He nodded, though he knew his curiosity would
make it a difficult vow to keep.

"Can we go back to the party now?" She swung
around, walked in the opposite direction. "I'll tell
you another secret if it'll make you feel better. But
you have to swear to keep quiet. My parents won't
like it if they know I told."

Judy smiled, rested her head on his shoulder.
"Remember I told you I asked for a car last summer? But Mom and Dad said no. I think they may
have changed their minds. Daddy said he has a surprise, a really big surprise, for my birthday. But I
can't tell anyone. Not even you."

Great. Judy was going to have her own car. And
he wasn't even allowed to drive his parents' except
on rare occasions. Why couldn't they be more lenient, like the Kings and the Wands?

They reached the pier, stood a moment beneath
the paper lanterns, and watched as several couples

danced to a song Peter didn't recognize. He'd never heard this particular band on KJIM.

LuLu came up as soon as she spotted them. "Ann-Marie cut the cake. She said to tell you she saved you a piece."

Judy held Peter's hand and walked with him toward the refreshment tables. They passed the bonfire on their way. Samantha sat at one end of a blanket, Carl and Ann-Marie on the other.

"Hey, buddy." Carl stuffed chocolate cake with vanilla frosting into his mouth. "Grab a plate and sit with us for a while. I'll give you a few pointers on playing pool. Maybe you can win your money back tomorrow."

"I'll be right there," Peter promised. But he was distracted, and surprised, a moment later when Samantha asked him to dance.

Judy encouraged him to accept. "Help take her mind off Becca," she said quietly.

Peter nodded. "I will, if the next dance is with you."

She kissed his cheek, and he waited until one song faded and another, slower one began to play before he held Samantha at arm's length.

He was careful not to step on her toes and tried his best to slide gracefully across the makeshift dance floor.

"I called Becca," she said. "But her parents must have had the line disconnected before they left on vacation. The recording said it was only temporary . . ." She giggled when Peter stumbled and nearly lost his balance. "I called another friend and asked her to deliver a message. Maybe Bec'll call tomorrow."

The party lasted until midnight.

No one missed Carl Tyrone until they needed his help to take down the string of lights.

Ann-Marie had cried so hard by the next morning that her eyes were swollen. She stood at the water's edge, with Judy and Peter, and tried to figure out how he'd slipped away without her noticing.

"I went by his cabin first thing this morning," as she had late last night, "but there's no sign he was ever there. Suitcases, clothes, everything's gone."

Judy had talked to the desk clerk and the manager before Peter had gotten out of bed. They told her the same as before, when Becca's family had checked out. They weren't given a reason why the Tyrones decided to leave. Only that they had. Late. Last night.

"I don't buy my parents' explanation." Ann-Marie strolled down the bank where Terry, LuLu, and Samantha had spread their blankets, though none of them was in the mood to swim or have fun. "Carl would never leave without saying goodbye, no matter how upset his dad was with the accommodations. I mean, one minute he was at the party. The next he was gone. There's something weird going on here and I don't like it."

Peter, though he didn't glance in his direction, felt Terry's steady gaze. They'd discussed Carl's disappearance over breakfast and Terry had made similar comments. Peter didn't want to believe the Tyrone's departure had been anything but what they'd been told. A spur-of-the-moment decision, something to do with Carl's dad getting upset and demanding a refund. Still, there were facts that couldn't be ignored. What were the odds of two people leaving the resort without so much as a farewell to any of their friends?

"Papa said Mr. Tyrone really lost his temper with the manager," LuLu said. "They nearly came to blows. Maybe Carl had to leave before his dad started a fight and got arrested."

Peter never thought he'd agree with her about anything, least of all this. "Could be. But that doesn't explain why none of us saw Carl leave the party."

They talked of little else that afternoon, though Judy tried several times to change the subject. Ann-Marie was inconsolable. By three o'clock she and Samantha had invented countless theories, most of them too bizarre to believe, why their friends had gone off without a trace.

After dinner none of them felt like doing anything special, so they hung around their cabins. Judy was in an especially pensive mood, and asked Peter if he would mind if she went in early, just after seven o'clock. She wanted to be alone, to try and sort through her thoughts. He returned to cabin 17 and found his mother on the couch, a damp cloth draped across her forehead.

"Another migraine?" Her complaints were more frequent and he worried that her aches and pains were more serious than just a headache.

His dad worked the crossword puzzle in the evening paper. "Margaret's all stressed out. Even a summer at Sinter's Cove can't help her relax."

"Stressed out about what?" Peter asked.

"Darned if I know." Perry Elton placed the newspaper on a table beside his chair, motioned for his son to join him outside on the porch. "I understand some of your friends are upset because the Tyrones decided to cut short their vacation.''

"Yes, sir." He didn't mention the theories that had been tossed about all day. His dad would call them ludicrous and suggest that Peter spend less time with people with such overactive imaginations.

"I'm going to tell you something. You can decide if you want to tell the others.''

His father sat on one end of the swing, Peter on the other. It had been so long since they'd had a heart-to-heart talk, he wasn't sure how to behave. He sat with his shoulders rigid, eyes straight ahead, and tried to prepare himself for the announcement.

"The Tyrones never planned to stay more than a few days. I only know what Reverend Anderson told me. How he's privy to the information is anybody's guess." His dad stretched out his legs, crossed them at the ankles. The chains creaked beneath his weight. "Carl and the McAnally girl were a little too serious to suit their parents. Ann-Marie's mother and father want her to attend college and get a job before she even thinks about settling down with a family. The Tyrones agree; they have high aspirations for Carl, too. They hoped it would be easier to break the news here than at home. Personally, I think that was a mistake. They should have nipped the relationship in the bud before they ever left town."

Peter didn't respond, didn't know what to say without losing his temper. It was a rotten thing for Carl and Ann-Marie's parents to do no matter how his dad explained the motives.

"Parents often have to make decisions they don't like. Mr. Tyrone went so far as to sell his house and apply for a transfer. Carl won't be there when Ann-Marie returns at summer's end.''

More bad news. The worst possible. He couldn't imagine how miserable Ann-Marie would feel, how he'd suffer if the same thing happened to him.

''You and Judy,'' his dad said.

He turned his head so quickly, he nearly sprained the muscles in his neck. He was afraid to hear what might come next. ''What about us?''

''You're not so serious you've discussed marriage?''

''No, sir.'' They were barely beyond the hand-holding stage. They kissed, of course. But Judy was too strict to allow him to become overly passionate. The thought of a serious commitment frightened her as much as it did him. ''I like Judy. A lot. But she has plans to attend MSU after graduation. She talks a lot about a career, but she's never once mentioned a husband, or kids, or anything like that.''

''I'm glad, son.'' His dad glanced toward the window where the living room lamp cast shadows across the porch. ''Now why don't you go upstairs and watch television. Keep the volume down. Your mother needs her rest.''

''Yes, sir.'' He opened the screen door and went inside. An evening of MTV would be a rare treat. Things would return to normal once he arrived back in Scarletville and that meant no TV except on those rare occasions when his mom watched a soap opera or his dad a weather forecast. Tonight he welcomed the distraction. Maybe he wouldn't think so much about Carl and Ann-Marie and the decision he had to make. He'd tell Terry the Tyrones' reasons for leaving. But Judy? She'd be heartbroken for Ann-Marie, the rest of her vacation ruined.

"Peter, darling."

He paused outside the living room door. His mother, still stretched out on the sofa, had her eyes open, her hand held in his direction.

He went to her, knelt on the floor, and started to kiss her cheek. But he was afraid that even that gentle a gesture would cause another bout of pain.

"Are you all right? Do you need something?"

"No." She squeezed his fingers, so weak he hardly felt the pressure. "I only wanted to tell you I love you."

"I love you too, Mother."

Her hair was sprinkled with gray. More than before.

There were liver spots on her hands. And deep wrinkles across her forehead.

She'd probably have a relapse once she looked in the mirror and saw how much she'd aged in the last few days.

EIGHT

Two more families checked out that week. By now people leaving was so commonplace that Peter hardly noticed anymore. Not everyone could afford to stay at Sinter's Cove all summer. Not every kid's parents had more than a one or two-week vacation. He half-expected to wake up some morning and find Judy gone. But only in his worst nightmares.

Terry spent so much time with LuLu that Peter rarely had a chance to talk to him alone. Carl's sudden departure, along with Becca's, put them all in a somber mood. Though every day they met on the beach and tried to make the most of their time.

"I'm bored," Samantha said. "Can't we do something different today?"

"Like what?" Terry asked.

"Suggest something." Judy was stretched out on her stomach beside Peter. Her skin, as dark as mahogany, was slick with oil. "We've swum. Boated. Hiked every inch of this stupid place. What's left?"

"We could climb the cliffs and look at the cove," LuLu suggested.

"No." Peter answered so quickly that everyone turned and looked at him. "It's too dangerous."

"That," Judy said, "sounds like a challenge."

"No." Terry backed him up. "Peter's right. One of us might get hurt."

"I want to see the cove." Ann-Marie closed her paperback. "No one told me there was a cove."

"Duh!" Samantha threw a chunk of ice from her Styrofoam cup, narrowly missing the other girl's shoulder. "This is Sinter's Cove. What'd you expect to find?"

"Do we have to climb the cliffs, or is there another way to reach the cove?" asked Ann Marie.

"We can swim around." Judy stretched and turned toward Peter, her eyes hidden behind dark glasses. "But I think I'd like to see the resort from the top ridge."

"You're hardly dressed for mountain climbing." Terry rose, removed his cap and tossed it onto the blanket. "None of us are. If we go, we rent a canoe."

"Takes too long and it costs money!" Judy was the first to reach the water. Peter waded in behind her and let the others get a good head start. Some of the other kids on the beach, including Quinton and Don, watched them leave but made no effort to join them.

"You never did tell me," Judy asked Peter as she waded in waist-high water. "What were you and Terry doing at the cove last week? What were you looking for?"

"Nothing."

"Liar."

He hadn't told her about Becca's ring, hadn't really thought about it again until just now.

"Terry found a piece of jewelry the day after

101

Becca left. A silver butterfly. We thought it might belong to her.''

Judy stopped, the water up to her shoulders. "Did it?"

He shrugged, tried to think of some way to change the subject. Why bring up Becca now, relive memories that were better left alone?

He swam out until the water was too deep to stand, and hoped Judy would follow.

She did, intent on continuing the conversation. "Terry found something at the cove he thought might belong to Becca. That doesn't make sense. Not when the last place any of us saw her was at the party.''

"We were wrong, Judy. Terry and I, like everyone else, were confused because Becca left so suddenly. We were eager to find some kind of explanation, so we jumped to conclusions. Chances are what we found belonged to someone else.''

"Where is it now?''

"Terry has it, I suppose.''

"I want to see, okay? I want to show Samantha, too.''

"Why?''

"If it belongs to Rebecca, she'll want it back.''

He dove below the surface, opened his eyes, and swam through the murky waters until he neared the cliffs. There were boulders strewn in the area and lots of rocks to step on and bruise his feet if he wasn't careful. Reaching the other side was safer this route, though still treacherous, and would probably take just as long as if they'd climbed the steep incline. Peter wouldn't have attempted to swim toward the center of the lake, away from the rocks or the bank on the opposite side even if he'd been alone. The distance was too great; there was always the chance he'd tire out or get a cramp before he could reach the shore again.

Samantha was the first to take a break. She climbed onto a ledge jutting out of the water and swept blond ringlets from her eyes. "I hope there's something interesting to see on the other side. This is a lot of work."

"There's nothing." LuLu blinked, tried to focus on the other girl. "I've been to the cove every night and it's hardly worth the trouble. I'll go back with you if you like."

Samantha refused her offer, and waited until Peter and Judy caught up before she set out again. She floated along the windswept waves, kicked her feet only enough to remain adrift, and dodged the moss-covered rocks that blocked her path. The water was too deep to stand, too dangerous to navigate at full speed.

Ann-Marie challenged Terry to a race as soon as she rounded the final bend, determined to reach the cove ahead of him or anyone else.

"You're right, Lucinda," Samantha said once she had a view of the canyon. "There's not much here. It's pretty. And peaceful. But I had hoped for a little more thrill."

Peter paddled behind Judy and saw the warning signs at the top of the cliffs, which he'd failed to notice at night. NO SWIMMING. NO DIVING. NO TRESPASSING. He'd have to try and talk the others into going back soon. His dad would throw a tantrum if his son were caught in an area of the resort that was off-limits to guests.

Terry helped LuLu across the stones and onto the bank near a pile of cattails. He waded back in

103

and followed the shoreline to another canyon wall where a clump of trees grew on the uppermost ridge. The best way for him to stay afloat was to grip clumps of grass and weeds and inch his lower body through the water.

"Where're you going?" Ann-Marie asked.

"Not far. I want to look around." He dropped below the surface, out of sight, and came back up a minute later.

"Show me where Terry found the butterfly," Judy said so that the others couldn't hear.

"Over there." Peter pointed the way. "In that pile of cattails."

Terry disappeared again, further down shore, and came up, spewing water. Reddish-brown hair draped over his eyes and blinded him.

Peter followed Judy across the stepping-stones LuLu had taken, ready to grab her if she slipped, and stood a moment later beside the dried reeds. The cove was dark and shadowy, not nearly as warm as the beach. Cool wind stirred the beads of water on his neck and shoulders.

"What're you guys looking at?" Ann-Marie asked.

"Nothing," Judy said.

Samantha joined them, looking over Peter's shoulder. "What's going on?"

"I . . ." Judy changed her mind at the last second, decided to wait and tell Samantha about Terry's discovery when they were alone. "Peter wanted me to see the cattails."

"You know how to show a girl a good time, don't you, Pete?" Ann-Marie studied the furry spikes in case she'd overlooked something interesting the first time, and returned to LuLu's side disappointed.

"Where's Terry?"

Lucinda leaned forward, eyes squinted against the dim light. "He went under a minute ago. He hasn't come up yet."

Peter joined them as soon as he heard the panic in Ann-Marie's voice. "Something's happened to Terry. Lucinda says he should have come up for air by now. Something's happened!"

He jumped into the water, oblivious of the jagged rocks, and made his way toward the clumps of grass where he'd last seen his best friend.

"Here?" he shouted.

LuLu shook her head, strained to see without her glasses. "Further down, I think."

Peter dove under, paddled as fast as he could, not able to see through the muddled water to know if Terry was there or not. He flailed his arms, hit only mud and rocks to his left, and continued to grapple for as long as he could while able to hold his breath. He surfaced only once, gulped fresh air, and went back under. He located Terry on the second attempt. Not yet unconscious, he was dazed, sinking rapidly toward the bottom. Peter didn't know what had happened, didn't care. He grabbed Terry around the neck with one arm—he'd never taken lifeguard training and didn't know the proper procedure—but knew enough that his friend would suffocate if he didn't get air soon. Terry was dead weight; fortunately he didn't struggle and drag Peter down too.

Finally, Peter managed to break the surface. Holding Terry's head above water, he swam toward the bank. Judy, Ann-Marie, and Samantha hauled him over the mud and grass and laid him beside the cattails. Judy was just about to start CPR when Terry coughed and spit water out of his nose and mouth. He blinked and looked around, stunned.

"What happened?"

"You tell us." Judy knelt beside him, out of breath.

"I was diving under. And I found a cave." Terry struggled to sit. "There must have been an undertow. The next thing I remember I couldn't find my way back."

"You shouldn't have gone off by yourself," Samantha said. "You could have drowned."

"Yeah." He leaned forward and blew water out of his nose. "You should've seen the size of that cave."

"Peter saved your life," Judy said.

Terry grinned as if it were an every day occurrence. "You were looking for some excitement. I guess you found it."

He had a cut on his forehead, not serious enough to require stitches, but one that would give him a bruise and a heck of a headache by dinner.

"Think you can make it back to the beach?" Peter knelt beside Judy, hands on his knees. Now that his heart no longer pounded and his adrenaline was back to normal, he was ready to return to the other side before anyone else injured themselves.

"Don't wanna go back," Terry said. "I want to check out that cave."

"You're crazy." Ann-Marie eased herself into the water, crawled over the nearest, largest rock, and dog-paddled toward the bend.

"You'll drown if you go back down there." Samantha grabbed one arm, Peter the other, and together they helped him stand. He was pale, his knees too weak to support him.

"All I need's a rope. I got a look—just a glimpse, really. But the cave's huge. Once you're inside, there's plenty of places to stand so you're not in the water. I'm telling you, we've got to check this place out before we go home."

"Not today." Judy led LuLu to the edge of the bank and they climbed down slowly, avoiding the rocks that were slipperiest. "You're hurt. Besides, this area is posted. We'll get in trouble if we're caught hanging around."

"Judy's right." LuLu waded up to her knees until she was certain that Terry would have plenty of help on his way back to the beach. "Mama and Papa have given me too much freedom for me to break their trust now. Besides, it's dangerous."

"Not dangerous." Terry allowed himself to be lowered into the water, then shook himself free of Samantha's grasp. He made his way toward the bend as if nothing had happened. "When we come back, we'll be better prepared," he told Peter.

"Man. You are crazy. You nearly drowned and you're already making plans to do it again."

"That cave was spectacular. No way am I going to miss seeing what's inside."

He went over the details so often, Peter was tempted to take him back and let him drown. He was glad when they reached the beach and grabbed their towels, hoping that maybe they could talk about something else now.

Terry stretched out on the blanket, flinched when Judy pressed an ice cube against his swollen forehead, and began to outline plans for his return to the cave.

First thing tomorrow morning, he said. He'd go alone if he had to.

"You're not going to let him out of your sight, are you?" Judy asked as she and Peter walked toward her cabin late that afternoon.

He shook his head, knew he was a fool for being as reckless as Terry, but there was no way he was going to pass up a chance to do a little exploring. Now that Terry's accident was only a memory, the risks didn't seem so great.

"If you're going, I'm going," Judy said.

"No way—"

"Think you're the only one who likes a little danger? I wouldn't be surprised if Samantha and Ann-Marie show up too. Lucinda I'm not so sure about. She's probably not willing to do anything to get her parents riled. I think they do more than just ground her when she gets in trouble."

The Wands hosted a cookout that evening. Bob Colby got drunk, embarrassed his wife, and left the party at a quarter till nine. Terry tried to act as if his dad's behavior didn't bother him, but he didn't look back as he walked with his parents up the hill toward their cabin.

"Likeable fellow," Reverend Anderson said. "It's a shame he drinks too much."

"Pity," Perry Elton replied. "Now if you'll excuse me, I should get home, too. Since my wife wasn't well enough to join us, I don't want to leave her alone too late. Come along, son."

"Yes, Father."

"See you tomorrow." Judy turned her back to the side yard, where her dad was shaking Perry Elton's hand. "Don't be late or we'll go without you."

Peter walked with his dad beneath the canopy of trees to cabin 17. He was glad they'd called it an early evening. As much as he wanted to be with Judy, he wanted to check on his mom, too. Her headache was gone, she said. But she didn't feel up to socializing just yet.

"Think Mother's going to be okay?" he asked.

"Sure." His dad strolled at a leisurely pace, hands in his pockets, the crunch of gravel beneath his leather shoes. "Let's talk about your birthday, son. It's just around the corner, you know."

"Yes, sir. Just around the corner."

Peter, against his better judgment, was the first to arrive on the beach the next morning. Terry showed up ten minutes later; Judy, Ann-Marie, and Samantha soon after.

The beach was deserted this early. There was no one to see them swim around the cliffs, no one to report them for going to a part of the resort that was off-limits.

"Are you sure you want to do this?" Peter asked.

"Sure." Terry, with a bright yellow ski rope coiled around his arm and shoulder and a water-proof flashlight in one hand, led the way. His forehead was swollen and bruised. He paid little more attention to his injury than if it were a mosquito bite.

Peter made his way to the cove. Swimming. Climbing. Crawling over slimy rocks. Judy was never out of his sight for more than a few seconds.

Ann-Marie and Samantha followed in a steady procession, both of them too nervous to exchange more than a few words.

Terry took charge once they reached the bay.

"I've got to figure out a way to tie this end of the rope at the top of that boulder." He struggled to pull himself onto the steep incline directly above where he'd gotten into trouble yesterday. But he couldn't manage alone. Finally, with Peter's help, he scaled upwards, with very little leverage and few toeholds to keep his balance. He stretched far enough to fasten one end of the rope around a cedar tree that looked strong enough to hold their weight. He slid back into the water, up to his shoulders.

He ducked out of sight, returned a second later. "Oh. Did I mention there might be snakes? So watch out for them, too."

Ann-Marie groaned, looked as if she might change her mind.

"It'll be okay," Judy reassured her.

Peter held the rope at the top of the waves until he felt a solid tug a few minutes later. "Terry's ready for us. Who's first?"

Samantha volunteered. She seemed only a bit nervous as she swam toward Peter and tugged at her braid.

"Be sure and pull on the rope once you reach the other end," he said. "That way I'll know you made it all right."

She nodded, waved at Judy and Ann-Marie, and held on with both hands as she slipped out of sight. She took twice as long as Terry to reach the cave, long enough that Peter thought she might have lost her grip and was caught in the crosscurrent. Just before he went in search of her, he felt the rope twitch between his fingers.

"She's down. Who's next?"

Ann-Marie went. Judy paddled out close to Peter and anxiously awaited her turn.

"I imagine the current's pretty strong," he said. "Sure you'll be okay?"

"If the others can make it, I can, too." She held his wrist, kept her balance in the water, and started down the rope as soon as Ann-Marie sent the signal that she'd reached the cave safely.

Watching Judy's long hair fan out above the blue-green waves and then disappear completely, he wished he'd never agreed to let her come. If something happened to her, he'd never forgive himself. Or Terry.

He let out a deep breath when he felt the cord jerk solidly against his palms. It was his turn and he knew now how the others felt. That moment of indecision. He was safe here. All he had to do was swim a few feet to the bank. What if something happened on his way down? What if he lost his grip, couldn't find his way back? He'd see the cave all right. Just before he drowned.

He filled his lungs with fresh air and went head first, pulling himself along the rope. The deeper he dove, the colder the water was. His vision was blurred. Once or twice it was impossible to see at all. He tightened his grip, made his way down the taut line. The undertow that had nearly swept Terry away yesterday was deeper than he suspected. He felt the waves swirl around his shoulders, tug at his hair. His fingers slipped and he held on more tightly with the other hand. The current was too strong, too swift. How any of the others had managed to hold on was hard to imagine. He felt his legs being pulled out, away from the rope.

Concentrate. He had to think about the other end

where Terry could help pull him to safety. He approached the mouth of the cave and was nearly through before he realized he'd come that far. Terry was right. The sight, though hazy like visions from a dream, was spectacular. The entrance was twice as large as any he'd seen before. He couldn't wait to view the cave from inside.

Strong fingers gripped his wrist, more than one person pulled him to the left. He rolled in the water and banged his knees against the jagged rocks.

"Dang." He was still blowing water out of his nose when Terry hoisted him onto a narrow ledge high above the steady stream that gushed through the opening.

"Didn't I tell you? Isn't this place great?"

"Yeah. Great." One wrong move and he'd tumble headlong into the water-filled chasm below. No way would he make it out of there alive.

Judy was safe. For that he was grateful. She huddled between Terry and Ann-Marie, her back pressed against the cavern wall. She looked relieved that she'd reached this far but too scared to go on.

The ledge was too narrow to pass safely. Peter shoved Terry out of the way and maneuvered around him so he could get to Judy. His bare feet gave him little traction, but he moved so quickly that he didn't have time to lose his balance.

"Still glad we came?" he asked as he knelt beside her.

She nodded, wet hair tangled around her face and shoulders. "Climbing back up that stupid rope's going to be fun, don't you think?"

Terry shined the flashlight over Peter's shoulder. The yellow beam sliced through the darkness, showed few details of what lay ahead.

"Wonder where it goes?" Samantha asked.

"Only one way to find out." Terry nudged Peter. "What'd you say? You wanna go first? Or me?"

"You're the one with the light." He pressed himself against the wall so Terry would have ample space to pass. Ann-Marie latched onto his arm the moment he started toward the cramped passageway.

"We'll only go a little ways, right? I mean, this place is huge. What if we get lost?"

"I have a keen sense of direction. We'll find our way back, all right."

Terry was determined to have a good time, despite the risks. It was impossible not to believe in—or have fun with—someone who acted so confident. Thankfully, the ledge widened a few yards away, onto a dirt floor with rocks strewn about. Ann-Marie and Samantha sighed in unison.

The opening, straight ahead, was so low that even Samantha, the shortest of them all, had to stoop so she wouldn't crack her forehead.

"I'm glad I'm not claustrophobic." Ann-Marie held Terry's arm and refused to let go, even though he struggled politely to break free.

The tunnel curved left; ahead was nothing but shadows. Peter was sure they would run into a dead end before they got very far and be forced to retrace their steps back to where they'd started.

The further they went, the lower they had to crawl to avoid the rocks overhead. The dirt floor gave way to mud and began a gradual slope upward. A few feet more and they were able to stand again, though even Samantha was in danger of

113

cracking her skull if she wasn't careful.

"Where do you think we are?" Judy asked. Her voice echoed through the darkness and died somewhere in the shadows ahead. "Have we come far enough that we're on the other side of the cliffs yet?"

"Doubt it." Terry trained the light left and right, up and down, never taking another step until he knew where it would lead. "But we're definitely more than half way."

So far there was little chance they could lose their way. Peter hoped the tunnel didn't take any unexpected twists or veer off into a series of other channels where they'd be forced to choose one way or the other. They could wander around for hours, lost like rats in a maze, if they weren't careful. He wondered how long it had been since anyone else had explored the cavern. Surely other summer guests had been as curious as Terry and had investigated the cove and found the underwater entrance, too.

"We can turn around any time you're ready," Ann-Marie said.

"Are you kidding?" Terry shined the flashlight in her face. "Don't you want to know what's ahead?"

"I do." Samantha, bravado regained, nudged the other girl and would have gone around if there had been enough room.

"What makes you think there's anything except more of the same?" Judy was, if not exactly bored, more than ready to go back to the area just before the ledge. At least there she had room to stretch her muscles. She shivered and Peter knew he wasn't the only one who was cold, cramped, and

114

uncomfortable. The air was so dank he found it difficult to breathe, to push away the panic that rose in his chest with every step. He wasn't claustrophobic, didn't mind close quarters, but it had been years since he'd dropped out of Boy Scouts and done anything this adventuresome. The ground was damp, and mud oozed between his toes—that was the creepiest sensation of all.

The tunnel veered left, dipped sharply down, and opened onto a tomblike area that Peter never expected. The room was half the size of his garage at home, but still spacious enough that he could move around and not bump into Judy or any of the others.

"Too bad we couldn't bring lunch," Terry said. "This would be a great place for a picnic."

"The only thing this place is good for is bats," Ann-Marie said. "There aren't any, do you think?"

"Nah." Terry didn't know any more about nocturnal flying mammals than Peter did, but he would have said anything to quell her fears.

They had traveled so far, that Peter guessed they were somewhere below the row of cabins nearest the beach. He wondered how long they could be gone before anyone missed them. Their parents wouldn't expect to see them until lunch. Quinton and Don might wonder why they weren't at their customary spots, catching a few rays the way they usually did this time of morning. Only one person knew where they were. Hopefully they could trust LuLu to keep their secret.

"I wish Carl was here," Ann-Marie said. "He'd get a kick out of this."

Judy quickly changed the subject. There was no sense in any of them becoming depressed because of the kids who weren't there to share the suspense. "What do you say if we don't find anything interesting in five minutes, we turn around and go back."

"Haven't you thought there might be another way out of this place?" Terry directed the flashlight so he could see Judy's response. Peter was momentarily blinded, he'd become so used to the darkness. "It'd be a heck of lot simpler if we didn't have to swim back."

"You're right," Judy said. "Only we don't know where we'll come out. We might have to hike for . . . I don't know how far. My feet hurt already."

"Don't buy trouble," Terry said, an adage he'd obviously borrowed from his mom or dad. "This tunnel can't go on forever. It's got to play out sooner or later."

"All right, then," Samantha said. "Can we rest awhile? My feet are sore, too, and I'm about to freeze to death."

"You'll keep warmer if you keep moving." Peter was ready to take a break, but he wasn't sure he wanted to linger longer than necessary. If Terry was wrong, and there wasn't a second exit, they'd have to turn around and go back. He wanted to save his energy to fight the current and pull himself back up the rope.

Terry moved to the far edges of the shadows, trained his light around the next corner. One tunnel veered right, another straight ahead.

"Please tell me your keen sense points you in the right direction," Ann-Marie said.

Terry grinned, tugged at the waist band of his swimming trunks. "Not exactly . . ."

"Then I vote with Samantha. Now's a good time to stop, rest, and decide what we want to do next."

Peter sat on the ground, back pressed against the damp wall, Judy on his left. Ann-Marie and Samantha found a flat rock large enough to accommodate them both and sat back to back so they wouldn't get their bathing suits dirtier than they were already.

Terry trained the yellow-white beam to his left, picked up a couple of small stones, and discarded them just as quickly.

"What're you looking for?" Ann-Marie asked.

"Something sharp to carve my initials. I at least want to leave a sign I was here." He disappeared around the corner and out of sight.

Peter knew the instant he returned that something was wrong.

"What?" He stood, brushed dirt from the back of his legs.

"There's someone else . . ." Terry placed his finger against his lips and motioned for them to speak quietly. "Just up ahead."

"Who?" Judy asked.

"Don't know. I heard a man's voice and hightailed it back."

"We're in deep trouble," Samantha said.

"Yeah." Terry glanced over his shoulder, listened for the voice, and turned back when he was satisfied that they were out of hearing range. "Wonder what they're doing down here."

"Looking for us?" Judy suggested.

"Not likely." Peter shook his head. "No one knows where we are."

"Lucinda does," Ann-Marie said.

"She'd never tell." Terry didn't care how defensive he sounded; by now everyone had guessed that he had a crush on the preacher's daughter. "She knows what would happen, she'd never say anything to get us in hot water." He switched off the flashlight and moved around the corner, but not yet out of sight. "At least we know there's no sudden drop-offs ahead."

"Where're you going?" Ann-Marie asked.

"I wanna know who else is prowling around."

"I'm coming, too." Samantha held up her hand, warding off any arguments. "I'll be quiet. I promise."

"It's best if we stick together, I suppose." Peter, despite his better judgment for the second time that day, walked ahead of Judy until they were in total darkness and forced to inch their way along the wall in single file.

He didn't dare speak, or hardly even breathe, for fear the slightest sound would reverberate and give away their presence. Still cold, damp rocks pressed against his neck and his palms were slick with sweat. His heart beat fast; every dull thump caused his mind to race with thoughts of what would happen if they came face to face with an employee. They'd be turned over to their parents, maybe asked to leave the resort. He'd be grounded for the rest of his life.

"Tell me again, daughter. Why did you insist we come this far when you haven't even washed the breakfast dishes yet?"

"I told you, Papa. I wanted to see the altar again. It's so exquisite. I've hardly thought about anything else since you first showed me."

"And the word of the Lord came unto me, saying . . . Ye mountains . . . hear the word of the Lord

God." Reverend Waymon Anderson strolled through the tunnel, a lighted candle to guide his way. "Your altars shall be desolate." Beside him was his daughter, baggy brown sweater to keep herself warm, her thick lenses reflecting the tiny, flickering flame. "And I will lay the dead carcasses of the children of Israel before their idols; and I will scatter your bones round about your altars. And ye shall know I am the Lord."

LuLu stopped suddenly, her gaze fixed on the darkness ahead.

Peter was positive she was about to tell her dad the real reason she'd brought him here.

NINE

"We'd better go back, daughter, before your mother starts to worry."

"Yes, Papa." LuLu hugged her Bible to her chest and returned the way she had come.

"What was that all about?" Judy spoke only when she was sure it was safe.

Terry knew LuLu better than any of them. But even he didn't have an answer for her bizarre behavior this time.

"At least we know there's another way out," he said.

"Yeah." Samantha slumped against the wall. She'd held her breath so long that her knees were weak. "But Reverend Anderson and Lucinda might be waiting at the other end."

Peter was still shocked, even a little scared. His thoughts focused in on one coherent fact. LuLu had known their plans, had definitely guessed they were in the tunnel, yet hadn't said anything to her father. Why bring him here unless she meant for him to know?

She'd said something about an altar. Who in their right mind would build an altar down here when there was a perfectly fine chapel with stained glass windows behind the clubhouse? LuLu's dad must have had his special place to pray too, the way his daughter went to the cove every night. Fanaticism, it seemed, was an Anderson family trait.

"What do you say, guys?" Terry asked. "Do we go forward? Or back the way we came?"

"Forward," Samantha said.

"Yes. I'm not sure." Ann-Marie looked at Judy, hoping for an answer.

"We'll have to be careful. No telling where we'll come out."

"Okay." Ann-Marie, her mind made up, grabbed the flashlight from Terry's hand and switched it on. "I'm ready to boogie. This place gives me the creeps."

Peter didn't have time to voice his opinion. He would have been out-voted anyway.

He walked in silence for a few minutes, at a slower pace than before, to allow LuLu and her dad plenty of time to get ahead. But not so far that their voices were impossible to hear. Reverend Anderson may not have known it, but his deep resonance, as he recited several more scriptures, led Peter and his friends through the dark the way a lighthouse guided sailors at night.

Judy purposely lagged behind the others. "What do you think Lucinda was doing down here, Peter?"

"I don't know. She said something about an altar." His feet had been punctured by so many rugged rocks and sharp pebbles that he thought his soles would never heal. "Maybe her dad sacrifices goats in his spare time."

"That's not funny!"

"Sorry." He should have known Judy wouldn't

find his humor funny under the circumstances. She'd taken a chance coming here, and was about to take a greater risk on her way out. She'd asked a serious question and he'd responded with an off-the-cuff answer.

"I wish I knew," he said solemnly. "LuLu's so strange I don't dare try and second-guess anything she does. I feel sorry for her sometimes. The kids at school make fun of her. But she brings a lot of it on herself. Spouting Bible verses, telling people they're gonna go to hell if they don't mend their ways."

"She can't help being a preacher's daughter."

"Father's a CPA. You don't see me cramming tax forms down peoples' throats all the time."

"It's not the same thing and you know it. You don't like Lucinda, fine. But you shouldn't call her names just because she has faith and you don't."

"Who says I don't have faith?"

Judy opened her mouth to respond, but decided she wouldn't. At least not to that comment. "I'm sorry. I don't mean to preach. But I feel sorry for Lucinda, too. I've only known her a short time, but never once has she said what she wants to do after graduation. I asked her the night of Carl's party, but she clammed up. Refused to talk about it."

"Maybe she doesn't know."

"I think she does. She just needs a few friends to push her in the right direction."

"I don't even know which colleges I want to apply to yet. How am I supposed to tell LuLu what to do?"

"Her name is Lucinda. And I wasn't talking about you. I was talking about me. And Terry." Judy swept her long hair over her shoulder, a sure sign that she wanted the conversation to end.

"Oh." He felt shut out, excluded from a part of her life because he was selfish and uncaring. "I'll try and be nicer from now on."

She smiled. Kissed his cheek. "You're nice enough most of the time."

Terry waited for them as they rounded the final bend.

"The exit's just ahead. Samantha and Ann-Marie have already gone through. Guess where?"

Peter shrugged. Judy shook her head she didn't know.

"The clubhouse basement. There's a wine cellar. The cave's hidden behind a door. Fortunately the Reverend forgot to fasten the lock on his way out."

Or LuLu left it open on purpose, Peter thought.

"How're we going to get back to the beach?" Samantha asked when Peter came out last, closed and locked the door behind him. "We can't very well go traipsing through the lobby in our swimsuits."

Peter led the way this time, through the wine cellar. The air here was almost as stifling as in the cave—and definitely just as cold—though there was enough light that he didn't have to worry he'd lose his way or run into anything unexpected. He climbed cement steps, opened a second door, and made sure there were no employees in the adjacent hallway.

In the basement, a maze of corridors wound their way beneath the ground floor. Somewhere distant, at the end of the hall, Peter heard the whirr of a washing machine and the thump-thump of towels tossed about in a dryer.

The second door to his right was unlocked. The

room, with a row of gray metal lockers against one wall, had two windows. One of them low enough so they wouldn't need a ladder to climb out.

Peter carried a folding chair from a desk beside the door that was so beat up and rickety, he was afraid it wouldn't hold his weight. Struggling to scrape away several layers of paint, he managed to open the antique lock and raise the sash. Thankfully there was enough foliage, including a trellis with ivy, to hide their escape. Just in case anyone happened by.

Peter reached down his hand and helped Ann-Marie onto the chair.

She smiled at Judy and Samantha. "You guys look a mess. I'm gonna take a shower and shampoo my hair. See you later."

"Yeah," Judy said, running her fingers through her tangled bangs. Her feet and ankles were muddy, her bikini covered with grime. "See you."

But she never did.

Ann-Marie was gone by the next morning.

"I was supposed to meet her for lunch but she never showed." Samantha sat on the porch of the cabin her parents had rented for the summer. "I never even had a chance to give her her card and gift."

"Gift?" Judy asked.

"Today's her birthday. She didn't want anyone to know because she didn't feel like celebrating. She had such big plans with Carl." She sipped iced tea and leaned back in the swing. "I saw her last night. She was going in the restaurant just as I came out. That's when her mom let it slip that Ann-Marie turns eighteen today."

"She didn't say anything about checking out?" Peter sat on the porch steps with Terry. Mrs. Owensby had served cookies with the iced tea. But none of them were hungry. Not even for home-baked chocolate chip.

"Not a word," Samantha said. "She wouldn't have made a date to meet me for lunch if she'd planned to leave Sinter's Cove."

Terry grabbed the wooden banister and pulled himself up. "This time it's different. Ann-Marie's in trouble. No explanation my mom or dad come up with will convince me otherwise."

"You're certain the McAnallys left?" Judy asked. "You asked the desk clerk?"

"Talking to her is like talking to a brick wall." Samantha pushed the swing back and forth. "The manager is even more tight-lipped."

"When Becca left, I didn't give her too much thought," Terry said. "Because I didn't know her very well."

"She's my best friend," Samantha answered. "I was stupid to think she'd go this long and not contact me unless she's in trouble, too. I've tried to reach her by phone every night this week, but her number's still disconnected. I'm tempted to steal my parents' car and drive home to see what the heck's going on."

"Carl's old man left the resort because he was unhappy." Terry adjusted his ball cap and stared at the afternoon shadows that stretched across the drive in front of the Owensbys' cabin. Their white Mercury was parked beneath a shade tree. "That sounded logical at the time. But I'm not so sure anymore."

"What're you saying?" Peter stood, too, his

voice so low that Samantha's mom, who was in the kitchen, couldn't overhear their conversation. "Our parents are lying?"

"It wouldn't be the first time," Terry answered.

"It would be for mine." Peter leaned wearily against the handrail. He was tired of arguing. Tired of trying to come up with reasons why so many families left the resort unexpectedly. None of the theories they'd discussed so far made sense. At least not to him. He couldn't—wouldn't—believe his parents would participate in a conspiracy that would endanger him or his friends.

"Your old man said he brought you to Sinter's Cove because it's your last summer at home. He's right. You'll be lucky if you make it back alive."

"Can it, will you?" Peter rarely lost his temper at his best friend. Sure, he'd gotten perturbed, lots of times. But never mad enough that he wanted to punch Terry's lights out for insulting his old man. He had better ways to waste his vacation than perched here trying to come up with reasons for Ann-Marie's sudden departure.

"I gotta go." He was halfway across the drive before he heard Judy's voice.

"What time is it, Peter?"

"Two o'clock. Ten till, anyway."

"I have to leave, too." She grabbed her purse and rushed down the steps to meet Peter. "I'll see you guys later."

"Yeah?" Terry grumbled. "Don't be so sure. That's what Ann-Marie said just before she disappeared."

"Cut it out, Terry!" Samantha was near tears, her legs folded beneath her as she huddled in a corner of the swing. "That's not funny."

"Where're you going?" Peter asked when he and Judy were on the main trail leading away from the cabin.

"To meet . . . someone."

Don Blevins. He knew without being told.

"Care if I tag along?"

"I most certainly do." She smiled, slipped her arm through his. "I'll meet you on the beach in half an hour. Bring a board game from the lobby. We'll lull away the afternoon, just the two of us."

Peter sauntered, alone, toward the picket fence. He glanced over his shoulder and watched as Judy headed to the pier, ebony hair shimmering with sunlight, legs dark and slender beneath khaki shorts. The last detail he noticed, just before she descended to the other side of the grassy slope, was her white sandals and how shapely and sexy her ankles looked.

She was late. By ten minutes. Peter rolled the dice again, moved three spaces to Park Place and looked up when a shadow fell across the paper money stacked in front of him.

LuLu glowered, eyes moving rapidly behind thick lenses. "Have you seen Terry?"

"Around two," he said, returning to his game, though it was really no fun when you owned the bank and your girlfriend was with another guy. "He was at Samantha's cabin."

LuLu sat on a corner of the quilt, uninvited, and remained silent for so long that Peter felt guilty for not at least attempting to make polite conversation.

"Are you enjoying your vacation?"

"Are you?" she asked.

"Yeah . . . everything's fine." Lucinda knew he

127

was lying. He could tell by the way she smirked and tilted her head so she peered at him over the top of her glasses. "We followed you and your dad out of the cave yesterday." There. He'd said it. If LuLu went to his parents, there was no way he could deny telling them what he'd just told her.

"You could've gotten lost. Or hurt."

"But we didn't. Thanks to you we found a safer way back."

"I wonder what Papa would have said if I'd pointed you out."

"But you didn't." He glanced up again, the game forgotten, and concentrated only on Lucinda. She might have been a lot of things—soft-spoken, shy, even a little strange at times—but he knew when he was being threatened. And he didn't like it one little bit.

She grinned, met his steady gaze, and refused to look away. "You owe me, Peter. Remember that. In case I ever need a favor."

He was glad when Judy finally showed, even if she was twenty minutes late. He knew the instant she settled down beside him that her meeting hadn't gone as planned.

"Everything all right?" he asked.

She nodded, smiled at LuLu. "How've you been, Lucinda? I haven't seen you around lately."

"Just fine, thank you." She retrieved the dice from the center of the board and tossed them out again. Double sixes. "I've never played before. Will you teach me?"

Judy answered before Peter could. Because they both knew what he would say.

"Sure. We'll be glad to."

And so his plans to spend the rest of the afternoon alone with Judy were sabotaged again. Instead he wound up bankrupt, losing all his hotels to the preacher's daughter on a final roll of the dice.

Terry sat at the dinner table while his mom spooned pudding into dessert bowls and his dad pounded a metal ice tray against the kitchen sink.

His parents had talked very little through the meal. He was glad; he wasn't in the mood to make idle chatter himself.

"We pay a king's ransom for this place and they can't even supply us with one decent ice tray." Bob Colby scooped several cubes from the sink, dropped them into his glass, and poured himself another shot of whiskey. "Good thing we didn't pay by credit card. I'd have cancelled the charges by now."

"Quit complaining, Robert." His mom slammed a bowl in front of Terry and another where his father had been seated minutes before. "I like the accommodations just fine. And so does Terry."

His dad looked over and waited for his son's response.

"Don't get me involved," he mumbled. The pudding was slightly scorched, but he ate it anyway, as fast as he could so he wouldn't be expected to talk with his mouth full.

His dad returned to his rattan chair, pushed his dessert out of the way, and wrapped both hands around his glass. "So, what've you been doing with your time, Ter? You're always running off with your friends. Your mom and I hardly ever see you."

"Beach," he said, hoping he wouldn't have to go into any details.

"Beach," his dad repeated. "I have to sell a crapload of cars to fund this little excursion, and all you can say is—"

"Eat your dessert." His mom sat with her spoon halfway to her mouth. "And leave our son alone."

"I'm just trying to have a little quality time. You're always telling me I don't spend enough—"

"I have a dictionary in my suitcase, Bob. Go look up the word quality and read its definition very carefully. You'll see you're way off base."

Oh, man. Terry swallowed the last mouthful of pudding and pushed his chair away from the table. This argument was headed toward one heck of a shoutin' match. He'd wind up in the middle if he didn't find somewhere else to hide.

He rinsed his plate, bowl, and glass, and was out the door before his dad could stop him.

"Is it too much to ask that you talk to your old man once in a while?" His dad strode from the room, drink clasped firmly in hand, and joined Terry on the porch. "Just a few minutes, son. That's all I'm asking."

His speech was slurred, eyelids droopy.

Terry swung away from the top step and plopped down onto the swing. He'd feel guilty if he left now and his dad were even more intoxicated, and in a worse mood, when he got back. Better to talk and get it over with.

"So?" His dad sat on the opposite end, as uncomfortable as Terry. "What's new?"

He wanted to laugh, his family life was such a joke.

"Not much, Dad. What's new with you?"

"I beat Pete's old man at golf today. You

should've seen him, Ter. He was so mad I thought he was gonna toss his clubs in the lake.''

Terry smiled, really wanted to chuckle this time. Mr. Elton's temper was legendary, especially when he was outdone at his favorite sport.

''You've been . . .'' His dad took a drink, leaned his head back, and closed his eyes. ''Avoiding me lately. Something on your mind?''

''Nah.'' His answer was instinctive—he had a lot he wanted to talk about—but why waste his time when chances were his dad wouldn't even remember the conversation this time tomorrow?

''We haven't done anything, just you and me, since we got here. What do you say, tomorrow we spend the whole day . . .'' His mind drifted. He took another drink, and frowned when the whiskey burned his throat. ''You got a birthday coming up. Seems like just yesterday you were running around in diapers and eating mud pies in the front yard.''

Another sure sign his dad's binge was going to be a humdinger. He rarely reminisced, but when he did, he became overly sentimental and wailed about wasted years and missed opportunities. His son was nearly grown. His only child didn't need his old man anymore. Terry had heard it all before and wasn't in the mood to listen again tonight.

He was tempted to leave. But he couldn't force himself to stand no matter how hard he tried. He looked at his dad, really looked at him for the first time in weeks. Drinking had certainly taken its toll. Especially since the start of their vacation. There were bags under his eyes. Not just dark circles, but purplish-black sacs that made him look like he'd been in a slugfest and come out a loser.

His jowls were flabby. Eyes bloodshot. Stomach

muscles deteriorated worse than a man twice his age. Peter's dad was in better shape and that, Terry found, disgusted him most of all.

"I don't tell you this often, son." His dad finished his drink and headed to the door to pour himself another. "But I'm proud of the way you've grown up. You're the darn best runner Scarletville's got. You bring home decent grades. I wish . . . wish . . ."

"What, Dad?"

"I wish we'd gone to Camp Hudgens."

He went inside. The screen door slammed closed behind him.

"Yeah," Terry said. "I heard the fishing's great this time of year."

TEN

Quinton Cullum never suspected a thing.

When he stepped out of his cabin the morning of June 27, they were all there to meet him. The Cavalier City High School marching band, cheerleaders, football squad, and most of the coaching staff.

"I can't believe we pulled it off." Judy stood near the front of the school bus, Peter on one side, Don Blevins on the other. The driver had been forced to park at an awkward angle because the road from the clubhouse to the cabins was too narrow, the ruts too deep to accommodate an oversize vehicle.

The band struck up a raucous rendition of "Happy Birthday" as Quinton was joined by his parents. They were even more surprised than their son, his mother in pink foam rollers, his father in a faded robe and worn house slippers.

Peter glanced over, saw the excitement in Judy's eyes. She was a great one for keeping secrets. Only she and Don had known that the group had planned to meet at the school gymnasium at six o'clock and ride to Sinter's Cove to help celebrate Quinton's special day.

"I couldn't have done this without you." Don leaned against the bumper, his crutches propped beside him within easy reach. "When I asked you to help me surprise Quinton, I never expected anything this elaborate. I wouldn't have dreamed it in a million years, much less known how to go about getting all these people together."

"No big deal." Judy smiled modestly, though it was obvious from the large turnout and enthusiasm of the Marchin' Cavaliers that she'd convinced someone that their cooperation would mean a lot to Don and Quinton. "I only had to make a few phone calls. Once the cheerleaders caught word I'd invited his teammates, they took over and contacted the band members. Quinton must be very popular. Not many kids I know would give up a day of summer vacation to ride in a crowded bus with no air-conditioning."

"You should've seen the manager's face when the bus stopped in front of the clubhouse and Coach Lonnie hopped out." Don was talking to Peter, the first conversation they'd had. "The manager asked Coach if he was lost. He wasn't going to let the band off the bus until I told him they were here by invitation. Mom and Dad were shocked too. First thing Dad asked was how much it was going to cost him."

"Nothing," Judy answered for him. "The kids volunteered their time and the coaches chipped in to pay for the gas."

"Quinton's been a real friend to me, especially since I hurt my knee." Don waved, gave a thumbs-up to one of the trombone players. "He came to see me every day in the hospital and three or four times a week while I recuperated at home. I'd have flunked if it hadn't been for him. He brought my homework and made sure I didn't miss any tests. I've probably blown my chances for a football scholarship. But thanks to Quinton and some of my teachers, I might still be eligible for an academic one.''

The band stopped playing and broke formation. The cheerleaders leapt into action, a special routine they'd worked out while en route to Sinter's Cove.

''I guess we'd better go,'' Judy said. ''We've still got things to do.''

Don grabbed his crutches and walked on one foot as Peter followed behind Judy. ''Our friends stopped on the way and picked up enough doughnuts for everybody. Judy talked the manager into serving orange juice and coffee outside the clubhouse.''

''I asked to use the restaurant or coffee shop,'' she said. ''But there are too many regular guests and he can't afford to close down for even an hour.''

Peter looked back, scanned the crowd gathered outside the Cullums' cabin. He didn't see Terry or Samantha. There were only a few kids from the resort present. Most of them were still asleep or having breakfast with their parents. Several others, more than half a dozen, had checked out since Ann-Marie. The large group that had attended Becca King's party had since dwindled down to only a handful.

LuLu stood in the road with her mother and father. Reverend Anderson didn't look pleased at the cheerleaders' short pleated skirts and tight sweaters, but he applauded when they ended one routine and went into another. An obvious favorite among the students of Cavalier, the whoops and hollers were so loud that Peter, Don, and Judy were forced to halt their conversation until they topped the next grass-covered slope.

Finally, Don swung around so that he walked beside Peter. "Thanks for letting Judy help me, man. She said she kept today a secret even from you. You knew we were meeting, but you didn't know why."

Peter nodded, tried to act as nonchalant as Judy had earlier. Now would not be a good time, he figured, to admit he'd been so jealous that he'd wanted to punch Don's lights out.

"If it had been me, I don't think I would have been so understanding." Don smiled, paused long enough to readjust the pads under his arms, and set out again. "A girl as pretty as Judy. Going off to meet another guy. I don't know how you . . ."

"I told you." Judy slipped her arm through Peter's. "Peter trusts me. He never once suspected I was doing something I shouldn't."

"Well," he admitted with a grin, "maybe once or twice."

When they reached the clubhouse steps, the kitchen staff had placed several tables on the front lawn near the fishpond.

The manager was nowhere in sight, but his assistant came over as soon as Judy had rounded the clubhouse porch.

"I think we've done a fine job on such short notice." He swept his hand toward the refreshments. "We could have done more if you'd warned us beforehand."

"We didn't want to ruin the surprise," Judy said.

"You're lucky. Mr. Meeker plans the staff's day down to the minute, and he hates disruptions of any kind. He wanted me to ask, do you have anything else planned to throw off his routine?"

"No." Judy smiled. "Nothing else. I promise."

"That was really fun." Samantha grabbed the last doughnut on a platter and helped Judy, Peter and Don stuff discarded napkins and cups into a plastic bag.

"Makes me miss my friends back home," Judy said. "I wonder what they're doing, what kind of fun I've missed this summer."

"Aren't you having fun here?" Don held the bag, balancing himself on one foot.

"Of course I am." She smiled at Peter across the table. "I'm with you guys, aren't I?"

Quinton was on the porch with a group of kids Peter recognized but whose names he didn't know. Quinton was barefoot, his shirt and cotton shorts wrinkled. The surprise had come so suddenly, he hadn't had time to dress or comb his hair. Brown wisps stood out from several cowlicks.

He stood as soon as Judy reached the top step. "I understand you're responsible for this. Thanks. I enjoyed seeing my friends."

"You're welcome."

"My folks told me not to make any plans this evening. They have something special lined up. But I was wondering . . ." He looked at Peter and Samantha, including them in the invitation. "Maybe we can all get together on the beach later. Mom and Dad aren't night owls. They usually watch the late news and go to bed right after."

"Sounds like fun," Judy answered.

Half an hour later, after the tables had been carried back inside and Peter had made sure there was no debris left on the front lawn, he joined Judy and the others at the corner of the clubhouse.

"I have to go." Don winked at Judy. "I owe you."

Peter had the distinct impression that he and Judy shared another secret. But he didn't ask. Judy wouldn't tell him anyway.

"So?" she said as she took his hand and walked toward the cabins. "What're we going to do for the rest of the day?"

"Whatever you like." Terry and LuLu were still by the fishpond, too involved in conversation to notice that they were the only ones left behind. "We have the whole day to ourselves."

Don expected his best friend to arrive at the beach by ten-thirty or eleven. At eleven-fifteen, he still hadn't shown.

No one had had time to arrange for a birthday cake—besides, there had been so many celebrations lately, that everyone was tired of cake—so Judy and Samantha had made a Boston cream pie in honor of Quinton's birthday.

Don sat on a log beside a small fire and poked at the flames with a branch left over from one of the previous parties. "Mr. and Mrs. Cullum ought to be in bed by now." He glanced at his watch, the third time in ten minutes. "Quinton should be here any second."

"It's a special night," Samantha said. She and Terry had wanted to cut the pie half an hour ago, but Judy had insisted that they wait for the guest of honor. "Maybe they made an exception because it's their son's eighteenth."

"Maybe . . ."

Peter kept a close watch on the time, too. He had strict orders from his dad to be in by midnight. "I hate to bust up the party." He stood reluctantly and smiled down at Judy. "I've got to get home."

"You have time to walk me, don't you?" She grabbed the pie from an ice chest. "We'll save this till tomorrow, I guess."

Don stoked the flames again. "Sorry Quinton bummed out on us."

"I'll make sure the fire's out," Terry said. LuLu hadn't been allowed to attend. She'd said that her parents were upset about something, but wouldn't go into details. Peter envied his best friend's freedom. Bob and Virginia Colby rarely gave their son a curfew. They trusted him to come home at a decent hour.

Peter barely had time to kiss Judy good night before he darted through the darkness, over the picket fence, to his own cabin. His mom and dad were in bed, the stairwell so dimly lit that he stumbled on the top riser. He'd turned back the comforter and kicked off his sneakers when he heard footsteps in the hallway.

"I thought it was time for you to come in." His mom stood outside the open door, her silk robe cinched around the waist.

"I'm a minute or two late," he said. "I walked Judy home."

"Doesn't matter." She shook her head. "As long as your father doesn't know." She lingered longer than Peter expected, staring at the moonlight outside his window, but not saying anything.

"You okay, Mother?"

"My blasted headache's gone, thank goodness."

"Did you have a good time tonight?" she asked.

"Yes, ma'am. Quinton didn't show. The rest of us built a fire and sat around and talked."

She lingered a little longer. Acted as if she wanted to say good night, but couldn't force herself to leave.

"That was quite a commotion we had this morning, wasn't it?" Her voice was suddenly serious, too serious for idle conversation. Peter was on the edge of the mattress, pulling off his socks. He looked up, afraid his mom and dad thought he'd had something to do with Don and Judy's plans and he was about to get in trouble for keeping secrets. "The adults were all abuzz this evening," she said before he could respond. "The Cullums had a confrontation with Judy's parents outside the restaurant. Seems they weren't too keen that their son's friends were invited without their permission. They said Judy had no right to plan how Quinton celebrated his birthday."

"She . . ." Judy would have been hurt if she'd thought the Cullums thought she was being disrespectful. "Judy only helped because Don Blevins asked her to. He's Quinton's best friend and—"

"I'm sure her intentions were good." His mother tightened her belt, glanced over her shoulder to make certain she wasn't talking so loud that she'd wake her husband. "Unfortunately, the Cullums don't agree."

"What did Mr. and Mrs. Wand say?"

His mother reached for the knob to close the door behind her. "I didn't hear. Your father ushered me away before I could eavesdrop. But I hate to see two families argue. They're so few of us left. We should all try and get along. Good night, darling. I love you.''

"I love you, too, Mother.''

He undressed, dropped his jeans and shirt on the floor beside his bed, and climbed between the cool sheets. Darn. It had been such a fun day. Now he had to worry that Judy had unintentionally insulted the Cullums. She'd no doubt apologize tomorrow, and hopefully there wouldn't be any further repercussions.

He tossed and turned until well after two o'clock and didn't go to sleep until he heard his dad go downstairs. Perry Elton rarely had trouble sleeping, but when he did, only a glass of warm milk helped him relax.

Hours later, a pillow landed on Peter's face. It might as well have been a bucket of cold water, it jarred him awake so suddenly.

He sat up, the top sheet twisted around his waist.

Don Blevins leaned against the footboard, one crutch supporting his weight. "Sorry, man. I know it's early. But . . .''

Peter rubbed his eyes and reached for his jeans. "Yeah, it's early. What're you doing? Something wrong?''

"Yeah. No.'' Don shifted his weight to the other crutch. "I'm not sure.''

"You're not making sense or I'm not awake yet.'' He slipped his shirt over his head and reached for his sneakers. "What time is it?''

"Eight o'clock. Quinton's mom and dad got into some kind of tiff with the Wands last night and—''

"I know,'' Peter said. "Mother told me.''

"I went to the Cullums' cabin first thing this morning. To apologize. Tell them it was all my idea, Judy was just helping me out because . . ." He adjusted the pads beneath his arms. "They're gone. At least I think they are. Mr. Cullum's car's not parked where it was yesterday. And the cabin's locked up. I must've really overstepped my boundaries if I made them mad enough to check out."

Peter was still groggy, but not so much that he didn't think about all the others. Becca. Carl. Ann-Marie. "They wouldn't be the first to pack up and leave in the middle of the night. Did you talk to the desk clerk?"

"No." Don headed toward the door. "I didn't think of that."

"Don't bother. It won't do you any good." Peter glanced at himself in the mirror, decided he didn't care if his hair looked as tousled as Quinton's had yesterday. He'd talk to Judy first, find out what kind of discussion she'd had with her parents, then come back later, shower, and change clothes. "Have you seen Judy yet?"

"I didn't want to face her without reinforcements. She's probably mad because I started all this in the first place."

"It was only a busload of kids," Peter mumbled. "What's the big deal?"

Judy met them at the door of her cabin ten minutes later.

"I can't talk to you." She forced herself to smile, refused to cry in front of Peter. "Dad's pretty upset."

"Darn, Judy. I'm sorry—" Don started.

"It's not your fault," she said. "It's nobody's fault."

"Yeah. But if you're in trouble with your folks, the least I can do is explain."

She shook her head and glanced over her shoulder toward the kitchen entrance. "I doubt they're in the mood right now. Dad said all sorts of things could have gone wrong yesterday. And I'd have been held responsible."

"I'll call Coach Lonnie. Make sure everyone made it home safe."

"You can't." Judy lowered her voice to a whisper. "All the phones to the cabins have been cut off at the switchboard. It's part of our punishment, I suppose. Some of the kids have been making long distance calls without permission and their parents talked to the manager. No more unauthorized calls unless we go through him first."

"That's the dumbest thing I ever heard." Don pounded his crutch on the porch.

"Judy," her mother called. "Your breakfast is getting cold."

"I have to go. I don't know when Dad plans to let me out. But I'll meet you as soon as I can. If you talk to Quinton, tell him—"

"We think he's gone." Peter shouldn't have told her, she already had so much on her mind. But Judy would get more angry if she found out later that he hadn't told her as soon as he'd suspected. "Try not to worry. I'm sure this whole thing will blow over soon."

But it didn't. Three days later, Judy was still confined to her cabin.

Peter was about to go nuts. Nothing Terry, Don, or Samantha said made him feel better.

"This thing's blown way out of proportion." Don leaned against the cedar rails of the Owensbys' cabin. "I've got to think of a way to set things right if it kills me. Mr. and Mrs. Cullum have always treated me like a second son. If I could just talk to them, make them understand Judy was involved because of me. Maybe they'd apologize to the Wands and everything would be okay again."

"Good luck," Terry said. "Your little stunt cut us off from the rest of the world. Even the pay phone in the lobby's been disconnected."

Peter and Terry were side by side on the steps, Samantha on the swing. None of them felt like going to the beach, hadn't been there since Judy's parents had grounded her. What had started as a great surprise wound up putting a damper on everyone's vacation.

"Another way, then." Don stretched, tried to relax the muscles in his arms and shoulders. The stress of the last few days was evident in his rigid stance. "I thought I had it figured out. But my parents said no. There's got to be something—"

"Said no to what?" Samantha asked.

He looked at Peter, started to answer, but didn't.

Peter found it hard to believe he felt pity for a guy he'd thought, until just a few days ago, was unfriendly and after his girlfriend. But Don Blevins had turned out to be a nice enough guy. He'd been sullen when he first arrived at Sinter's Cove, he said, because his doctor had told him the day he'd left Cavalier City that he might not play football next season. He'd come to accept his injury, the inconveniences of crutches, and no longer went around with a giant chip on his shoulder. Quinton, he said, had helped talk him out of his bad mood.

"No to what?" Samantha asked again.

"I can't tell you," he answered. "I promised

Judy." He looked at Peter again. "Don't get on my case. It's not what you think."

Peter shrugged. The jealous thoughts were definitely back. "What am I thinking?"

"I'm sneaking around behind your back, trying to put the moves on your girlfriend. Judy would kill me if I told you anything else."

"She'd have to see you first," Samantha said. "And who knows when that will be."

Don kept quiet a moment, stared toward the woods across the road from the cabin. "Judy promised to help me with Quinton's party. And I promised to return the favor. Only now my parents won't let me."

"What were you supposed to do?" Terry asked.

"I . . ." He hesitated again. "It has to do with Peter's birthday. I can't tell."

"You can if it means I can see her again." Peter pulled himself up and strode across the porch. "None of us will tell Judy. And I'll act surprised no matter what. Now talk."

"She went to the mall in Scarletville," he began reluctantly. "To buy your birthday present." He nudged the tip of his crutch with his sneaker, refused to look at Peter. "Something she really wants you to have. Only the store didn't have it in stock. They had to special order and . . ."

"And what?" Peter prompted him.

"She's upset because it won't be here in time for your birthday. So I told her I'd borrow Dad's car and drive to Scarletville. I didn't think to ask Mom or Dad first. I just told Judy I would if she'd help me surprise Quinton. Only now I can't. I think my parents know I'd swing by to see the Cullums and try to straighten all this out."

Don's hometown was less than an hour's drive from Scarletville. He could have made it to both places and back to Sinter's Cove in one day, no problem.

"I feel guilty Judy kept her promise and I can't."

"Don't worry," Peter said. "She'll understand. My birthday's not for another couple of weeks. We'll think of another way to get my gift here if we have to."

"Yeah." Terry stood, bored, ready to do something other than sit around. "We'll take my old man's car. He won't mind."

"This gift of mine," Peter asked, "when's it supposed to be ready?"

Don slipped his crutches under his arms and walked to the edge of the stairs. "I don't know. Judy was going to let me know as soon as she heard from the bookstore . . ." He stopped, pounded the porch with the rubber tip of a crutch. "Darn. I knew I'd say too much if you kept asking questions."

"So we know it's a book." Samantha rose from the swing and grabbed her tote bag from a table beside the door. "Why can't the publisher or the store just drop a package in the mail?"

Don eased down one step at a time. "Who knows? I don't know all the details."

"I'll talk to her." Samantha bounded past Don so quickly he almost lost his balance. "Her parents will probably let her see me before they will any of you."

"You can't. Judy'll know I ruined her surprise."

"What's the big deal?" Terry was at the edge of the drive, anxious to leave, though neither he nor Peter knew exactly where they were headed. They'd spent the last three days just sitting around, worried about Judy, and wondering what they could do to help. But their hands were tied, whether they liked it or not. The Wands had confined their daughter to cabin 4 and nothing anyone said—especially Peter—was going to change their minds.

"I told you, we'll take my old man's car to the mall in Scarletville. Pete'll have his book and Judy won't mind who you told as long as it's here in time for his birthday."

Samantha lingered at the edge of the drive, her heavy bag hoisted over her shoulder. "I'll let you know what I find out. Meet me on the beach. I know it won't be much fun. But I'm not going to waste another afternoon sitting around, doing nothing."

"Amen." Terry waited until Don caught up before the three of them left the Owensbys' cabin and walked toward the pier. "Mind if we go by Lucinda's cabin first? I haven't seen her since last night. She might want to go with us."

"Sure." Peter's day was ruined already. Sharing LuLu Anderson's company was no worse than not being able to see Judy at all. He glanced over his shoulder and watched as Samantha ascended a grassy slope, her blond braid swaying side to side. He looked at the Owensby cabin again. Samantha's mother was at the threshold, only her silhouette visible through the screen door. Someone else stood at the corner of the porch. At least he thought they did. He couldn't be sure; he caught only a glimpse. When he looked again, the shadow was gone. And Mrs. Owensby had retreated back into her cabin.

ELEVEN

Peter slept on a beach towel, his T-shirt rolled up as a pillow. Don had wandered down the bank twenty minutes ago, to the cliffs at the north end of the beach. Samantha and Terry swam most of the afternoon, taking short intervals to reapply sun screen and work on their tans.

Peter drifted in and out of sleep, the sun warm against his back, the sounds of waves breaking against the muddy shore lulling him toward dreams. He heard Terry's laughter and Samantha's threats to drown him if he tried to dunk her one more time.

"Peter?"

He heard a voice. Knew he wasn't dreaming.

When he opened his eyes and rolled on his side, LuLu stood at the end of the towel, Bible clutched at her side.

"Are you awake?"

"Yes." He pulled himself up, still groggy, and reached for a smaller towel to wipe sweat from his shoulders. His hair was damp, the waistband of his blue trunks wet with perspiration. There were few other kids on the beach, no one within fifteen feet of him and LuLu.

She looked toward the lake, made certain Terry hadn't noticed her arrival and was about to approach in time to hear her conversation.

"Remember when I told you you owed me a favor."

He nodded, a lump in his throat. LuLu was so glum; whatever she was about to ask had to be serious.

"I remember. What do you want?"

"You can't let Terry go to Scarletville."

"How'd you know . . . ?" The shadow he'd seen beside the Owensbys' cabin. "You should have told us you were there instead of eavesdropping."

"You can't let him go," she said again.

"Why not?"

"Convince him he can't ask his dad to use the van. No one can know he wants to leave Sinter's Cove. Least of all his parents."

"Tell him yourself. Once Terry makes up his mind, nothing I say matters."

"If you care about Terry you'll do what I ask." She left before he had a chance to respond or ask what the heck she was talking about. So Terry wanted to drive to Scarletville and he planned to use his dad's van. No way would Mr. Colby say no; he never had before.

Samantha raced ahead of Terry, her swimsuit soaked, and retrieved a towel draped over her tote bag. "Beat you!"

Terry grabbed his cap, pulled it on. Beads of water trickled down his neck and shoulders. "Where's Lucinda going?"

"I don't know." She'd come and gone so quickly, and her conversation had been so cryptic, that he felt as if he'd dreamed the whole episode.

"She didn't stay long." Terry was puzzled. And more than a little suspicious. "What'd she say?"

"She knows you're planning to go to the mall as a favor to Judy."

"How?" Samantha looked at Terry. "Did you tell her?"

"No. We went by her cabin earlier but her dad said she was busy in the kitchen and wouldn't let me talk to her."

"How'd she know, Peter?"

"She overheard us." He didn't mention she'd hid around the corner and listened intentionally. "She said you shouldn't go." He tried to make the comment casual, but the words made even less sense than when LuLu had said them. "She said your dad shouldn't know that you want to leave Sinter's Cove."

Samantha tucked a few loose strands back into her braid. "I still don't understand how she knew Terry volunteered to go. Unless Don—"

"Unless Don what?" He lowered his crutches beside the towel and sat next to Peter.

"Have you talked to Lucinda today?" Samantha asked.

"Lucinda who?"

"Terry's girlfriend."

"She's not my girlfriend." Terry grabbed his shirt, used it as a towel, and dried the beads of water off his shoulders. "I like her, okay? But her old man's a preacher and he hardly lets me near her."

"Whoever she is, I haven't talked to her." Don stretched his injured leg out, rolled his foot from side to side. "I haven't talked to anybody today except you guys."

"If she's not your girlfriend, why is she telling you where you can't go?" Samantha smirked. Terry had teased her most of the afternoon and she'd found the perfect opportunity to pay him back. "You're not going to let her get by with it, are you?"

"Of course not. I'm going to Scarletville. And that's final."

"Sorry, son. I have to say no this time."

"What?" He'd purposely waited until eleven o'clock, to allow his dad plenty of time to get drunk and agreeable to just about anything, before he'd asked to use the van. Judy had told Samantha that the book was in and ready to be picked up any time. He figured asking permission was just a formality, anyway. His dad always let him use one of the family vehicles whenever he wanted. Heck, they had a car lot full.

"You're joking, right?"

"Afraid not." Bob Colby leaned back in the swing, his glass of ice and whiskey resting on one knee. "And if I were you, I wouldn't mention we had this conversation to your mother."

He'd waited until she'd gone to bed, because he knew she'd find excuses why he shouldn't go. But he'd counted on his dad being on his side, depended on him to convince his mom that she was a worrywart and her son was mature enough to make the trip. He'd driven to track meets all over the state, most of the time with only Peter.

"I can leave early morning and be back by afternoon. I'll just go to the mall and that's it. I promise."

His dad didn't answer. He downed his drink in

one long gulp and pushed the swing into action. The wooden slats creaked, the only sounds for a long time.

"Ter," his dad said finally. "You've got to understand. My hands are tied." He stared straight ahead, his eyes wet with tears. "I can't let you leave the Cove."

"Bull!" He was in no mood to be mollified. If his dad was going to cry in his beer tonight, he'd do it alone. Terry moved from the swing so suddenly, the chains sagged and his dad's head was jerked to one side.

"Where're you going, son?"

"Pete's," he said as he took the wooden steps in a single bound. But he had no intention of disturbing Peter's family this time of night. Old man Elton would have his head. He headed instead to Don Blevins' cabin. He'd knock on the door only if there were a light in the window.

"We've got it all worked out," Terry told Peter at breakfast the next morning.

Don pushed his plate away and drank his second glass of milk. He'd eaten three eggs, two orders of bacon, hash browns, biscuits and gravy, and a short stack drowned in syrup. The coffee shop waitress refilled Terry's cup, asked Peter if he wanted anything, and moved to the next booth when he said he didn't.

"There's a kid here this summer named Virgil." Don leaned forward, lowered his voice so no one else in the room could hear. "You might have seen him around. I don't know him very well. I've only talked to him a couple of times myself. But he's kind of a rebel, you know. I thought if anybody's willing to sneak his parents' car, it'd be him. So I asked him last night and he said yeah, no problem."

"You can't be serious." Peter looked across the table and hoped Terry was smiling, that this was all a big joke. His best friend had done a lot of crazy things, Peter had even gone along more often than he liked to remember, but neither of them had ever planned anything this risky.

"I thought I might ask if I could go with you. But not if—"

"Yeah." Terry said. "I figured you'd say that."

"We're going, Pete. With or without you." Don fished in his jeans pockets until he found enough cash to pay his check.

Terry reached for his wallet.

"My treat," Don said as he slid his crutches toward the chair. "Save your money for gas."

None of them spoke again until they were through the lobby, off the clubhouse porch, and on their way down the grassy slope toward the pier.

"Getting to Scarletville and back's not a problem." Don had gotten so expert with his crutches, Peter hardly noticed a change in his own pace. Only when they reached a slight incline did Don slow up so the rubber tips wouldn't slide and throw him off balance. "The thing is, we're going to Cavalier City, too. We can hit the interstate back, so it'll take an extra hour and a half, maybe two, depending on how long it takes me to convince Mr. and Mrs. Cullum that Judy's being punished for something that's not her fault."

Peter walked a few more feet, realized Terry was waiting for him to respond. His best friend still hoped he'd changed his mind and go with them.

But there were too many reasons why he shouldn't. He couldn't find a reason good enough to convince him to get involved with a kid who'd steal his parents' car for a joyride. Terry was about to defy his parents in a big way, and Peter had never done that once in his life. He hated to consider the consequences if he did. Because they'd be caught. No way could three or four kids sneak away from the resort for hours and not be missed. And the Cullums were sure to tell Don's parents that he'd showed up at their house when he was supposed to be at Sinter's Cove.

"You guys are gonna get in trouble because of my stupid birthday," he said. "It's not worth it. Judy will be disappointed, sure. But she'd be the last person who'd want you to do something this—"

"I'm not doing it for Judy." Terry tugged on his cap. Something in him had changed since yesterday. His best friend was reckless, even a little wild at times. But Peter had never seen him so hell-bent on disobeying his parents.

"Why, then?" Peter had to ask. The camaraderie they'd shared was strained, their friendship in jeopardy. If he knew Terry's reasons, he'd have a better chance of talking him out of it.

"This summer is a ruse, buddy," he said. "I told you before we left Scarletville, something's not right. Maybe I was just guessing then. But I'm sure of it now. The only way I'll know what is to talk to someone who's been here and left."

"Quinton." Don nodded in agreement. "I've got to know he's okay. Too many weird things have happened. I hadn't really noticed until Terry pointed them out. People leaving in the middle of the night. Kids going to parties, there one minute, gone the next. My parents have always let me come and go as I please. But it's like they're keeping me here against my will. It's an odd feeling and I don't like it.''

"Don't you think you're over—''

"Don't tell me I'm overreacting,'' Terry said stubbornly. "That don't wash, not like it did in the beginning. We were given lame excuses when Ann-Marie and Carl left, and Rebecca too, and I bought them. I even accepted that Quinton's parents took him home and Judy's folks grounded her because they got into it over a lousy surprise party. But last night . . . last night was the clincher.''

"What happened last night?'' Peter asked.

"My old man told me no. And that, no matter how you look at it, ain't normal.''

They reached the picket fence and Peter climbed over, the way he usually did when he came this route, before he remembered that Don had to go further down, to the gate, before he could get to the other side.

"Sorry,'' he mumbled. His mind was definitely somewhere else. Like how to convince Terry he was about to gamble, big time, and lose. He sensed—felt a vibration stronger than any he'd known before—that Terry was headed for big trouble. Peter had a lot of experience at being told no; surely there was something he could say to soften the blow. Make Terry understand that his dad had his reasons, and none of them were as sinister as he wanted to believe.

Anything he said, he knew, would be pointless. A waste of breath.

Terry was going to Scarletville and nothing could stop him.

There was only one other person on the beach this early. The long-haired kid in his favorite shirt, a picture of Jerry Garcia emblazoned across the front.

"Pete, meet Virgil," Don said. "This is Peter Elton."

Virgil nodded, motioned for them to sit beside him on the pier. He looked as rough and unfriendly as he'd been the night of Rebecca's party.

"You're right. Something's going on. Dad always keeps a spare key in a little metal box with a magnet on the back. He's real absentminded, my old man. He's locked his keys inside so many times it's not funny. Only I checked and the key's not there."

Peter laughed, started to tell them they were off the beam. How could they justify stealing a car and lying to their parents because of something as insignificant as a key? Only he didn't say anything. Because he knew it wasn't just Virgil's parents. Or Judy's. It was Terry's. And his own. Everyone was entitled to change a habit or two, alter their behavior from time to time. But what were the odds that everyone at Sinter's Cove this summer would take extra precautions to keep their children from leaving? He might not like Terry's and Don's plan— might not agree it was the right thing to do—but he was beginning to understand why they thought it so important to talk to Quinton.

"I talked to the doorman this morning," Terry said. "He said the Fourth of July cookout starts at eight P.M. It's usually adults on one end of the lake,

156

kids on the other. Then they all get together for the fireworks display at ten.''

"That should give us time to get to the mall in Scarletville, over to Cavalier City, and back here before our parents miss us,'' Don said.

Peter had been daydreaming, so wrapped up in his thoughts that he'd missed an important part of the conversation.

"I thought Virgil didn't have keys. How are you going if—''

Virgil turned, his ponytail—tied with a rubber band—draped down his back. "Where've you been, man?'' He was a smart aleck, cocky, the kind of guy Peter would have stayed away from if he'd attended Scarletville High. "I told you I slipped the dishwasher fifty bucks to let me use his car.''

"The dishwasher!'' Judy would never believe how much trouble Don was going to just to keep his end of the bargain. "How in the world did he get involved?''

"I figure he works for minimum wage. If anybody needs the extra cash, it'd be him.''

"You don't know this guy from Adam, but you trust him not to tell anybody where you're going just because you pay him off?''

"I'd do it for fifty,'' Virgil said. "Why shouldn't he?''

There were a hundred reasons why, but Peter didn't have an opportunity to voice even one. Terry spoke up before he could.

"All right, it's settled. We leave day after tomorrow. There's a noon picnic. As long as we make an appearance, then slip off, no one should know we're gone.''

Day after tomorrow. July 4th. There would be a

full day's schedule after lunch. A golf tournament, volleyball, horseshoes, boating, swimming, skiing. Chances were Terry and the others wouldn't be missed as long as they were back by ten o'clock, since their parents would be so busy celebrating Independence Day.

"Since you're not going, you can cover for us if anybody asks," Virgil said.

"Sure," Peter said. It would be a lie, but it was the least he could do for his best friend.

He sat silent, his legs over the side of the pier, as Terry, Don, and Virgil went over their plans again. Virgil had arranged to meet the dishwasher on a side road a short distance outside the main entrance.

Peter didn't speak again until he was alone with Terry. There were other kids on the beach, though the water was still too cold to swim. Samantha, if she stuck to her routine, would no doubt arrive in the next few minutes.

"It's not too late to change your mind," Peter said.

Terry leaned forward, looked at the waves below his sneakers. "You understand why I have to go, don't you?"

"No. You'd never have thought of it if it hadn't been for Judy."

"Maybe not. But as I said earlier, I'm not doing it for her. I'm going because of Ann-Marie and Carl and—"

"Don't forget Rebecca." Peter meant it as a joke. But her absence only darkened the mood.

"Her too. I have to know why they all left so unexpectedly. Talking to Quinton's our best bet. If he's okay, chances are the others are too. But if he's not—''

''Hi, guys.'' Samantha approached the end of the pier, her tote bag slung over her shoulder. ''I take it Judy's folks still have her grounded. Otherwise she'd be here.''

Peter nodded.

''They'll let her celebrate the Fourth, I'm sure. No one can be that mean.''

None of them would have guessed she'd be grounded this long. So much had happened—so much was about to happen—Peter had given up trying to second-guess anybody's next move. The Wands had their reasons for keeping Judy sequestered in their cabin. She might not be allowed out for days . . . weeks. There was only one good thing. She was still at Sinter's Cove.

Their other friends had not been so lucky.

TWELVE

The evening of July 3rd, Peter stayed at the Colbys' cabin until a few minutes before his curfew. He and Terry talked, not about anything important, and certainly not about tomorrow, but chose instead to discuss everything from Latin to track to which of the SHS cheerleaders was the prettiest. Just like they usually did, always had before, until the last few weeks. Peter wished he could forget about tomorrow, would give anything if he could talk Terry out of going. But he didn't try, made no mention of the trip. Plans were made, and gone over, so there would be little chance they'd be missed. Peter would do what he could to cover with their parents until they got back. But he'd avoid Bob and Virginia Colby. He could lie to them once and get by with it. But twice, and they'd probably get more than a little suspicious.

"I'd better go. Don't want to be late." He moved to the stairs and glanced back at Terry on the porch swing. "See you tomorrow."

"Yeah," he said as casually, as if it were just another day. "See you tomorrow."

* * *

Terry went inside a few minutes after Peter had left and grabbed a soft drink from the refrigerator. His dad was in the living room, his mom already in bed. They'd had another argument and hadn't spoken to each other since yesterday.

Nothing new, he thought as he undressed and slipped between the cool sheets. He drank his Coke, belched, and thought he'd probably have trouble sleeping. His mind tossed with thoughts of tomorrow and what would happen if their plans went awry.

He fell asleep half an hour later.

There was a hand clasped firmly over his mouth when he opened his eyes again.

"Ter, buddy." His dad was on the edge of the bed, fully dressed, including his red and white windbreaker from the booster club. "Don't say anything. Don't make any noise. Okay?"

He wished the heck his dad would move his hand so he could breathe again.

Bargainin' Bob Colby moved toward the door. "I want you to get dressed. Fast. We're getting out of here."

Terry glanced at his alarm clock next to the empty Coke can. "Darn, Dad, it's two o'clock in the—"

"Shhh! You'll wake your mother."

Terry pulled the sheet up over his waist and closed his eyes. "Go back to bed. You're drunk."

"I've never been more sober in my life. Get dressed and meet me downstairs."

Terry ignored him. His old man had talked about going fishing or camping, but this was ridiculous. It was the middle of the night, for chrissakes. Not a good time to get soused, overly sentimental, and decide on a father-son outing.

He sat up only when his dad shook his shoulders so hard he nearly bit his tongue.

"Terry. I'm serious. I want you to get up."

He leaned nearer, his face only a few inches from the pillow. There was no liquor on his breath, none of the putrid fumes Terry had gotten so used to over the years that he hardly noticed them anymore.

His dad was sober. And he meant business.

Minutes later, he was dressed and at the bottom of the stairs. The wooden door was open, the screen unlatched. He eased outside, careful not to push the door too wide. The hinges squeaked, and his mom was a light sleeper.

His dad waited inside the van, key in the ignition.

"Get in, son. And don't slam the door."

"Where're we going?"

"I'll explain later. Right now, all you need to know is, we're leaving. And we're not coming back."

"Peter," Terry started, but his dad interrupted him before he could finish.

"Sorry, son. I'm not brave enough to save you both."

"What do you mean?" He climbed in the passenger seat, closed the door with only the slightest click. His dad started the engine and backed from the drive to the rutted road that would lead them past the clubhouse. To the main gate. And onto the highway.

"Why do you mean, save us?" he asked again.

But his dad never had a chance to answer.

Ahead, blocking their path, were three men. Reverend Anderson, Perry Elton, and Mr. Wand.

His dad stomped the accelerator, tried to run them down, but swerved to the left at the last second. The van careened toward the picket fence and the golf course beyond.

Terry closed his eyes, braced himself against the floorboard, and prepared himself for one hellava collision.

"Big doings today," Perry Peter Elton III said from behind his newspaper.

Peter finished his glass of orange juice and wiped his mouth with a paper towel. "Yeah. Terry and I have got our day pretty well planned. I hope you and Mother don't mind that I won't be spending a lot of time with you until the fireworks show."

His mother sipped her coffee, forced herself to smile. "Of course not, dear. Your father will be on the golf course most of the day and Mona Wand and I have plans of our own with some of the other mothers."

"Will I see Judy today?" he asked, and held his breath.

His dad folded the paper and placed it beside his plate. "I wouldn't count on it. Joe says she's only made matters worse by constantly questioning why she was grounded in the first place. Every time she asked, her mother added another day. At last count, she won't be allowed out again until next week sometime."

"But her birthday's in three days."

"Save your breath, son." His dad held up his hand. "I have my hands full with you." He looked at his wife across the table and smiled, something he hadn't done until he'd come to Sinter's Cove. "I'm not about to start telling other people I think they're too strict with their children."

Peter went to the coffee shop, expected to find Don in the middle of another huge meal. His mom hated to cook, he'd said, and would rather pay someone to make sure her son ate a balanced diet.

But there was no sign of Don. Or Virgil. Or Terry.

He searched everywhere he could think of and stopped by Samantha's on his second trip back to Terry's cabin.

She met him at the door in jeans and a blue and white sweater. She'd not yet braided her hair and made him wait on the porch while she went back upstairs.

She came out several minutes later, hair tied with a festive red, white and blue ribbon. "Happy Fourth of July," she said.

"Yeah. You too."

"Wonder where they've gone." Samantha reached the end of the Colbys' drive first. And noticed right away something Peter had missed the first time. The Colbys' van was not parked where it had been since the first day of their vacation. No wonder no one had answered the door when he was here before.

They went to the clubhouse, waited thirty minutes, and made the return trip to the row of cabins.

Samantha climbed the porch steps, started to settle down on the swing and wait, but changed her mind.

"I know you don't want to hear this. But . . ."

She peeked in the window, trying not to be too obvious. "Maybe they checked out."

"Terry would never leave without—"

"That's what I said about Becca. Remember?"

Peter didn't care if he were caught peeping or not. He leaned as near the window as he could, shaded his eyes from the morning sun, and tried to see the interior of the cabin. Peter saw that the television was on.

He tried the screen door, found it latched from inside, and pounded louder than he had before. Someone was inside. No way could they ignore him this time. And he wouldn't go away until he talked to Terry or his mom or dad.

Virginia Colby opened the door, dressed in a chenille robe—pink with red roses—her hair wrapped in a towel. Only a few wet strands were visible on her forehead.

"Good morning, Peter. Have you been by once this morning? I thought I heard someone earlier."

"Yes, ma'am." He had a lump in his stomach—though at least he knew the Colbys hadn't checked out—but he wouldn't feel completely at ease until he saw his best friend face to face. "I was looking for Terry."

She removed the towel, dried the ends of her hair. "Sorry I didn't make it downstairs in time before. I was still asleep when you knocked."

"That's okay, Mrs. Colby. Is Terry home?"

"No." She stepped outside, saw Samantha and smiled. "Didn't he tell you? Bob volunteered to drive Terry to Scarletville. Something about an emergency trip to a bookstore. I tried to get them to wait until tomorrow. But you know how stubborn they can be. Imagine going all the way back home for—''

''When did they leave?'' Peter had already backed toward the stairs and would have run over Samantha if she hadn't moved out of his way.

''This morning some time. Bob told me good-bye, but I was so groggy I didn't look at the clock.'' She folded the towel over her arm, leaned against the cedar rail. ''I'm sorry. Did you want to go with them? It was such a spur-of-the-moment trip, Terry probably never thought to invite you.''

''Yeah. You're probably right. Thank you, Mrs. Colby.''

He exited as quickly as he could, and didn't stop again until he was on the main trail leading away from the cabin.

''She's lying.''

''How do you know?'' Samantha asked.

''Terry would have told me if there was a change of plans. I don't care how spur-of-the-moment. He wouldn't have gone off and left me hanging.''

Samantha walked beside him, grabbed his hand, and made him stop. ''What do we do now?''

''Terry planned to go to Scarletville, all right. But not with his dad. He and Don—and a kid named Virgil—paid to use a car. They were going to leave sometime during the picnic. I don't know exactly where they're supposed to meet the dish-washer, but I'll be there in Terry's place. You'll have to cover with my parents, Samantha.''

She gripped his fingers more firmly. ''Slow down. I'm confused. Especially about the dish-washer.''

Peter took a deep breath, tried to calm his nerves. ''It's his car they were going to drive to Scarletville and Cavalier City.'' He had to think clearly if he expected to pull off such a wild scheme. Terry's parents might not wonder where their son was if they didn't see him until nightfall. But Margaret Elton's little boy was never given more than a couple of hours before he had to check in. "I have to find Don and find out where they're supposed to meet. It has to be close. Don can't walk far on crutches.''

The picnic started at eleven-thirty. By ten minutes till noon, there was no sign of Don or Virgil or any of their parents.

"They're not coming,'' Peter said. Something was terribly wrong. But he didn't tell Samantha, didn't want to upset her more than necessary.

"I made sure Mom and Dad saw me,'' she said. "I told Mom I was going to hang out with you for the rest of the day and I wouldn't see her again until the cookout. It's three hours to Scarletville and three hours back. If Terry and his dad haven't been at the mall by the time we get there, we'll know for sure Mrs. Colby lied.''

"Not 'we,' Samantha. I can't ask you to—''

"You didn't ask. I volunteered. Besides, I'm ashamed I didn't think of it weeks ago when Becca disappeared.'' She dumped her plate, most of the fried chicken and potato salad uneaten, and joined Peter at the fishpond again. "Let's go. We've got to figure out a way to get off the grounds without anyone seeing.''

Peter discarded his own plate, waved at his mom on the porch of the clubhouse, and walked with Samantha along the trail toward the lake.

"We can't back out now, Peter.'' She slipped

her arm through his, the way Judy did. He missed her now more than ever.

He tried not to appear too conspicuous as he glanced over his shoulder, made sure he was out of sight of his mother. His dad was on the golf course and might not stop for lunch at all.

"I haven't seen Lucinda today," Samantha said. "I wonder where she is."

Peter didn't answer, didn't want to think about the preacher's daughter. He had more important things on his mind.

He topped a short incline, made sure no one was headed in the opposite direction, and darted left, Samantha in tow. She was too short to climb the wire fence alone, so he helped boost her over. In seconds, the foliage was too dense for them to be seen by anyone who happened along the trail.

He walked slowly, careful not to step on a twig or piles of dead leaves. They were still near enough to the resort that someone could hear them if they weren't quiet.

It took longer than he expected to circle north, and west again, and come out on the main road which led from the highway to the rustic gate with cedar letters overhead.

Samantha was out of breath, but too nervous to take a break. "Which way now, do you think?"

He made certain no one was in the area, no unexpected vehicles on the road, before he set out on the shoulder. He could dart back into the woods, hide behind a tree in split seconds. He could only trust Samantha to be as alert.

"There's a road there," she said. "On the left."

He nodded, followed her lead, and found the

dishwasher five minutes later standing beside his blue Camaro.

"Hi." Peter approached cautiously. Virgil had arranged for the car. The black-haired man in white trousers and stained shirt might not trust anyone else with the keys. "Virgil sent me to get your car."

"Who's Virgil?" He leaned against the open door, dark eyes darting from Peter to Samantha and back again.

"The guy who paid you fifty bucks."

He seemed to relax. But only a little.

"The deal was, he'd meet me. Why'd he send you?"

"There's been a slight change in plans. Nothing major."

"I don't know..." He stared at Samantha, looked over her shoulder to make sure there was no one else coming down the road.

"Look, you already have the money." Peter glanced at his watch. He didn't want to push the dishwasher too hard and cause him to back out of the deal. But he didn't want to spend a lot of time dickering, either. Time was wasting, and they had precious little to spare. He reached for his wallet. "If it would help convince you, I'll kick in another..." He counted the bills quickly.

"Make it another fifty," the man said. "You've got a deal."

"Twenty." Peter held out the money. "It's all I have."

He put it in his shirt pocket.

Samantha didn't have her tote bag. But she immediately began to dig in her pockets. "I have a little money."

"Keep it." The dishwasher climbed behind the wheel. "You'll need it for gas."

Samantha and Peter got into the backseat, Peter on the passenger side.

"You can drop me off at my sister's trailer and pick me up when you come back. You gotta be there before nine. I work tonight. Everybody works tonight."

Three hours to Scarletville, three hours back. And it was just now twelve-thirty.

"No problem," Peter said.

The dishwasher turned left after a couple of miles, drove only a short distance and parked in front of a mobile home with a junked Volkswagen and childrens' toys scattered in the front and side yards.

"Be careful with my car, man. You wreck it, it's gonna cost you a lot more than fifty bucks."

"Seventy," Peter reminded him, and slid behind the wheel.

Samantha was so petite she could climb over the seat with no difficulty. "Remember, if anybody asks, you never saw us."

Neither she nor Peter spoke again until they were on the interstate, driving only a few miles above the limit. Getting ticketed by a state trooper was really the least of his worries. He had to get there and back as fast as he could. Before his parents missed him.

"Peter." Samantha turned toward him, as far as her seat belt would allow. "I hate to ask. But I'm a little nervous and . . . well, I had a big glass of tea before we left. Do you think we can stop? Not now—it's not an emergency yet—but in a little while?"

He exited at the same truck stop where he'd eaten lunch with Judy and her parents on the day he'd arrived at Sinter's Cove. He pumped gas while Samantha went inside the station to pay and to use the ladies room.

She climbed back in, handed him a soft drink and candy bar.

"I don't know about you, but I'm starved."

They didn't stop again until they reached Scarletville.

"I have to go by my house before we hit the mall," Peter said as he took the first off-ramp. "It's not too far out of the way."

"Okay." Samantha stared out the window. But her curiosity finally got the best of her. "Why?"

"I'm broke and I want to buy Judy a present while I'm here. Her birthday's Saturday."

"I'd loan you some, but I only have a few dollars myself. Allowance is not till Friday."

"Mine too. Fortunately I haven't robbed my savings in a couple of months." Hopefully he could get in and out before Samantha realized he kept his spare change in a pink papier-mâché piggy bank he'd had since his first year at summer camp.

He didn't realize how much he'd missed his neighborhood until he turned south off Jockey Avenue and headed toward his house three blocks away on Ruby Lane. The first thing he noticed when he rounded the final intersection was the bright yellow and red sign posted near the mailbox.

"What the . . . ?"

FOR SALE. SHOWN BY APPOINTMENT ONLY.

"What's the matter?" Samantha asked. He'd hit the brake so hard, she was jerked forward, spilling what little Dr. Pepper she had left into her lap.

He couldn't answer. Was positive he'd taken a wrong turn, maybe made a mistake, he was in such a big hurry. Only he knew that was impossible. He could have found his house blindfolded.

"You look like you've seen a ghost," Samantha said.

The two-story house where he'd lived all his life. For sale? His parents would never do that, not without discussing it with him first.

He pulled into the drive, parked in front of the garage. And was out the door before the engine had completely shut down.

He was at the porch, key in hand, when another thought struck him. This was just the kind of stunt Terry would pull, the kind of practical joke he'd plan so his best friend would have a surprise when he returned from vacation.

Yeah.

He felt better.

Unlocked the door.

And stepped inside the empty foyer.

"What's going on?" Samantha was directly behind him. She walked through the empty hallway, into the empty living room. "I thought you lived here." Her voice echoed through the bare rooms.

"I do." He rounded the corner, went through the dining room into the desolate kitchen. Gone were the walnut table, black and white television on the counter, cat clock above the back door.

He almost ran over Samantha on his way upstairs.

His bedroom furniture was gone. No clothes in the closet, no piggy bank atop his chest of drawers.

Samantha was leaning against the newel post when he returned.

"We're in trouble. All of us." He thought for a moment his knees were going to buckle, that he'd topple headlong onto the hardwood floor below. "Judy. Terry. We've got to get back to Sinter's Cove."

He was on the porch, doorknob in hand, when he remembered the last time Judy had visited him here.

"I'll be right back."

He bounded up to the second level, two stairs at time, so fast his sneakers almost slid out from under when he hit the floor where a rug had been the day he'd left on vacation.

The attic door was unlocked, the room stripped of its contents.

The photo album was still in the crevice, between the sheetrock and studs, where he'd dropped it the day Judy had surprised him.

THIRTEEN

"What's that?" Samantha asked when she saw the red binder.

"Pictures." He tossed the album into the backseat. "I brought them because they're the only thing left." He backed from the drive, narrowly missing the mailbox, and headed toward Murrey Avenue.

"Where're we going, Peter? I thought we came in the opposite direction."

"We did." He sped as fast as he dared without attracting the attention of any police officers patrolling the neighborhood. Unlike the highway patrol, they wouldn't just give him a ticket and let him go. They'd release him only to the custody of his parents.

He parked in front of Judy's house ten minutes later.

"No For Sale sign," he said. "Thank goodness."

"Then maybe it's not as bad as we think." Samantha didn't sound at all convinced.

"Terry was right from the start." He shifted from neutral and was about to continue on to the next intersection when a white station wagon turned the corner behind him. "Mother and Father wanted me out of town so they could sell the house and I wouldn't know. But why? Where are we going to live when we come back from Sinter's Cove?"

His mind reeled with possibilities, none of them good.

He waited until the station wagon pulled ahead before he eased his foot onto the gas pedal and moved a few feet alongside the curb. He slammed the brakes again when the station wagon pulled into Judy's driveway.

A woman with short hair, as black as Judy's, went to the passenger door to help a toddler unbuckle her car seat.

"Excuse me." He was out of the car before Samantha could stop him.

The woman turned, startled, ready to protect herself and her daughter if she thought he meant them harm.

"Excuse me," he said again, gentler this time. "But the Wands are on vacation."

"Yes," she said cautiously. "I know. The real estate agent told me when I rented the house."

"You live here?"

"We moved in three weeks ago, my husband and I. And Meagan, of course." She smiled down at the dark-haired girl at her side. "We were lucky to find such a big house for lease in Scarletville. Especially since we don't know how long before my husband's next transfer."

"Then the Wands aren't coming back?" Peter asked.

"No. At least not here. That's what the real estate agent told me."

175

Peter headed to the interstate, cursing traffic when it moved too slow and red lights when they changed too fast. There was no need to drive to Terry's house. He was sure he'd find a realtor sign or another family camped out in the Colbys' living room. And though it was only a few minutes past four o'clock, and they were right on schedule, he didn't go to the mall, either. His book and Judy's disappointment were the least of his worries.

"Peter?" Samantha had been so quiet, Peter so lost in his thoughts, he'd almost forgotten she was in the car. "What do you think's going on?"

"I don't know." He clutched the steering wheel, finally reached the on-ramp, and wished he were headed anywhere except back to Sinter's Cove. Only he had to return. Judy was there. And Terry. And maybe by the time he returned the Camaro to the dishwasher, he'd have figured out what his parents were up to and how to stop them.

The sun began to set by the time they passed the truck stop. Their conversation had been limited; Samantha spent most of her time staring out the window. Only once did she mention her home and wonder if the same thing was happening to her that had happened to Peter and Judy.

He pulled in front of the mobile home after dark and honked the horn. When there was no response, he gave three additional blasts.

"Leave his stupid car here and let's walk," Samantha said.

"It's too far." He shifted gears and made a sharp U-turn. "We'll leave it on the side road. He'll know where to look when we don't show by nine o'clock."

"We shouldn't have to sneak back through the

woods, should we?'' Samantha asked. ''Most everyone will be at the lake by now.''

Peter nodded in agreement. It was too dark to go traipsing through unfamiliar territory. He didn't want to take the chance that one of them would get a snake bite or sprain an ankle.

He turned off the headlights, dropped the keys in the ashtray, and set out with Samantha toward the Cove.

''Are you going to ask your parents why they're selling your house?'' she asked.

''I can't afford to. They'll know I went to Scarletville and . . . I want to talk to Judy first.''

''I haven't heard from Becca since she left. Do you think she's okay?''

He took so long to consider the question, to try and think of exactly the right way to answer so he wouldn't frighten Samantha any more than she already was, that he was nearly at the gate before she stopped. And grabbed his arm.

''Do you, Peter?''

''I came back because I'm not sure any of us are safe,'' he answered honestly. ''If it wasn't for Judy and Terry, I might have kept going.''

''Why didn't you go to the police?''

''And tell them what? Mother and Father are selling my house and I don't like it. There's no law against that.''

''We could tell them about Becca and the others.''

''They might not take a missing person's report from us. And even if they did, it could be weeks before they track them down.''

''So? What are we going to do?'' Samantha

crossed through the open rustic gate, glanced up at the cedar letters above.

"I don't know. Yet."

They kept close to the shoulder, avoided the clubhouse the best they could until they were able to walk freely along the path. Several people passed in the opposite direction. No one paid them any attention.

"Word would have gotten out by now if our parents reported us missing," he said. And breathed easier than he had since early that morning.

"I want to go by my cabin first," Samantha said. "I'll meet you at the pier."

"Okay." He'd gone only a few steps when she came back and grabbed his arm again.

"Daddy calls me his little princess. And mother cries every time I talk about moving to New York after graduation. She worries about me when I'm five minutes late coming home from a date. Why would someone who does all that want to hurt me?"

"I don't know." He'd accused Terry of jumping to conclusions. He wouldn't be guilty of the same. But there was definitely something going on that shouldn't be. He had proof, more than enough. Now he needed to find his best friend, talk to Judy, and decide what to do next.

"In the meantime." He wrapped his arm around Samantha's shoulder and knew she wouldn't misinterpret the gesture. They'd been through too much not to share a special bond. This, he thought, was how it felt to have a sister. "I want you to be extra careful, okay? If you suspect something's not right—"

"Like what?" she asked nervously.

"Becca and the others turned up missing overnight. If you suspect your parents are about to check out—if you think there's the slightest chance you might be leaving—you've got to get word to someone. Okay? Promise me."

"I'll do the best I can."

"See you in a little while," he said as he headed toward his cabin. He'd make a quick pit stop before he headed to the lake and the cookout.

"See you." Samantha waved over her shoulder.

But he didn't see her again that night.

Peter bounded up the stairs to cabin 17, opened the door with his key, and started upstairs. He expected his parents to be at the lake, chowing down on barbecue. But they weren't. He'd taken only one riser when he heard muffled sounds from the living room.

"Peter?" His mother's voice. "Is that you?"

"Yes, ma'am." He eased across the foyer, peered into the adjacent room. She was on the sofa. She'd been crying—not just teary-eyed and mawkish—but so shaken that her hands trembled, her face looked as pale as the moon outside. Deep wrinkles were furrowed across her forehead. "What's the matter, Mother?"

"Where have you been, son?" His father stood beside his favorite chair, hands in his pocket. "We've been looking for you since six o'clock. Where were you?"

"With Samantha Owensby. We—"

"Peter, why don't you have a seat."

In the chair, partially hidden behind Perry Elton, sat Reverend Anderson. Peter hadn't noticed him until now.

"Your parents and I have something to tell you."

"What?" He eased onto the cushion beside his mother. She reached out at once, took his hand, and squeezed his fingers.

"There's been an accident," his dad said. "Terry and his father were driving back from Scarletville. There was a collision on the highway. A terrible pileup from all accounts. It happened about four-thirty."

About the same time he and Samantha had left Bledsoe County. They would have seen the accident if there had been one.

"Bob Colby's dead," Reverend Anderson said. "God rest his soul."

Peter stood, spoke before he could stop himself. "You're a liar."

"Son." His dad placed a firm grip on his shoulder. "I know you're upset. But that's no excuse to insult people and call them names. I want you to pull yourself together and . . ."

Peter shook himself free. Never before had he been less afraid of his father's wrath than he was at that moment. "Next you'll be telling me something's wrong with Terry, that he's in a hospital somewhere, so I won't wonder what really happened to him. Well, it won't wash this time. I know what's going on."

He sat on the window ledge, one sneaker pressed against the floor, and watched the fireworks light up the night sky. Red, blue, and silver rockets soared high above Lake Andrew Sinter amid a blaze of sparks and high-pitched whistles. Peter turned away before the bombs burst. Before the showers of red and white embers drifted toward the waves below.

The explosions rattled the window panes behind him.

He had two windows, had tried to raise both sashes soon after his father had locked the bedroom door. But the panes were solid sheets of glass, sealed from inside, and impossible to open. He'd been angry enough—and scared enough—to consider tossing a chair through the tinted glass. But he knew his parents and Reverend Anderson would hear the commotion and stop him before he managed to escape very far.

He sat on the edge of his bed. Listened to the muffled sound of explosions outside, heard the cheer of the crowd. And knew the fireworks display would reach its finale soon.

Try as he might, he was still too shaken up to remember every detail that had happened just after he'd called Reverend Anderson a liar. He'd accused his father of lying, too. About Terry. And Bob Colby. He'd tried to leave through the front door, to get to Judy, and reached the porch steps before he'd been subdued and forced back across the threshold. He still didn't know who he'd struggled with—his dad or Waymon Anderson—but supposed it didn't really matter. He was a prisoner, the way Judy had been ever since the day after Quinton's birthday.

He stared at the doorknob for a long time. Knew it would be a waste of energy to walk across the room, a waste of time to try the lock. He had to think clearly, plot another way to get to Judy and find out what had happened to Terry. Because he didn't intend to stay here for days. Or even through the night, if he could figure a way out.

Mr. Colby was dead. At least that's what his dad wanted him to believe. But nothing was said of his best friend's condition. And Peter hadn't had time to ask. He'd been too busy trying to leave.

Only now he wanted to know. Terry was still alive—he'd told himself that so often, he believed it as strongly as he believed he'd find a way out—otherwise he'd be tempted to crawl between the sheets and give up till morning.

Terry was in trouble. Definitely in danger. So were Judy, Samantha, probably every kid at Sinter's Cove this summer. The only way any of them could escape was to help each other. But how could he, when he was locked up, and couldn't even save himself?

He was still on the bed an hour later when he heard footsteps on the stairs. Heard his father's muffled voice outside the bedroom across the hall. His mother was there, footsteps soft, words filled with anguish.

"How can you sleep at a time like this? How can you expect me to do anything but pace the floor?"

"Our son was out of control, Margaret. He'll be better by morning. Now come to bed."

"Not until you unlock that door and let me check on Peter first."

"Margaret . . ."

Peter eased across the room, careful that his footsteps were silent, and pressed his ear against the door. His parents were no longer on the top landing. At least not his father. His mother was near the door, her voice barely audible.

"You promised things wouldn't be any different

this time. You swore coming to Sinner's Cove ahead of time wasn't a mistake.''

"Sinter, Margaret."

"Why don't you just admit it? You and Waymon made a mistake. Peter's outsmarted you, but you're too bullheaded to . . .

". . . shut up, Perry. I'm going to have my say this time and you're not going to interrupt me until I'm finished. Things were different eighteen years ago. Little Meg was much more timid and would rather have had her right arm cut off than stand up to you the way Peter did tonight. She was a beautiful child, but not nearly as bright . . .

"I didn't say she wasn't smart. I only meant she lacked the sophistication that's so inherent in children today. We've tried to keep Peter away from computers and television and all sorts of modern technology. But for all of our efforts, he's still more savvy . . .

"Hang his Latin grades, Perry! I was able to say good-bye to Meg and all the others because they were totally unsuspecting until the very end. I know it makes little sense, but their innocence is what I've carried with me each time we started a family. But I've known Peter was different from the time he was old enough to walk . . .

"You're wrong, Perry. You might have been able to bully your son so far. But tomorrow, when you have to look at him across the table, you're going to understand what I'm talking about. We've lost Peter's trust. So many others have failed over the years and you called them naive, unfit parents. I wonder. What are you going to say when the same thing happens to you?''

She closed the door and the cabin fell silent.

Peter slept very little that night.

He kept hearing his mother's voice—"Little Meg . . . each time we started a family . . ."—and wondered if he'd overheard the conversation by accident or if she'd intentionally spoken loud enough for him to listen through the closed door.

He knew now who the pink and white dresses in the attic belonged to. A sister he'd never known. There had been others, too. Siblings whose names he'd never heard, faces he'd never seen.

Except perhaps in pictures.

He sat cross-legged on the mattress, back pressed against the headboard, a pillow hugged in his lap. He hadn't taken his eyes from the door since sunrise. He'd retrieved the photo album long enough to toss in the back seat of the Camaro. Where he'd promptly forgot it. Because he'd had other, more important things on his mind.

He could only hope the photographs were still there. That the dishwasher hadn't noticed the red binder and tossed it out the window because he was late for work and mad at Peter for not parking the car within walking distance of his sister's dilapidated trailer.

The lock swung free some time after seven o'clock. He saw only the top of his father's silver-white hair as he peered through the opening.

"Your mother's started breakfast. You have time to shower and dress before you're late."

Thirty minutes later, his mother set a plate in front of him, filled his juice glass. She had as difficult a time as Peter in pretending that everything was okay, that this was an just another day, an ordinary meal in the Elton household. She sat across

184

the table, drank her coffee, and refused to make eye contact.

Finally, his father folded his morning newspaper, placed it in his lap. He had not spoken since Peter had entered the room.

"Son, you have an important decision to make. Either we leave the Cove today or we stay until you're ready to apologize for your insubordination."

Peter didn't respond. He'd been through enough of his father's lectures over the years to know he was expected to remain silent until given permission to speak. Not to defend, or even explain, his actions. Merely to accept whatever punishment his father deemed appropriate.

Only this time it was different. He had to convince his father for Judy's sake, and Terry's, not to leave the resort.

"I'm sorry."

His father glared at him. Shook his head. Drummed his fingers on the placemat.

"You'll tell the Reverend the same, of course."

Peter nodded.

"Then perhaps we'll get on, enjoy what's left of our vacation." He pushed his chair away from the table, walked to the door. And turned back. "But you understand, of course, you're grounded."

"Oh, Perry," his mother started. "Don't you think you're being a little too—"

"You're grounded until I say otherwise. That means no visitors, no television . . ."

Peter bit his lower lip. He wanted to laugh, shout, cry. Anything to make his dad realize how ludicrous this conversation was.

"Sure, Father," he wanted to say. "You're sell-

185

ing our house right out from under me. You're lying to me, keeping me from Judy and Terry. But darn, do I have miss MTV, too?"

His dad retreated to the living room. His mother immediately began to wash the breakfast dishes.

Peter slipped away unnoticed, went to his bedroom, decided he'd rather be anywhere but there, and went back downstairs again.

"Father?"

Perry Elton glanced up from his crossword puzzle. "Yes, son?"

"May I sit on the porch?"

"You'll go no farther?"

"No, sir."

"And you won't talk to anyone?"

"No, sir."

"All right. Half an hour. And then I want you back inside."

"Yes, sir."

He'd been on the porch swing only a few minutes when he heard someone behind him, at the corner of the cabin.

" ' . . . fools despise wisdom and instruction. My son, hear the instruction of thy father, and forsake not the law of thy mother.' "

"Shut up, LuLu." As much as he needed help, as desperate as he was to get word to Judy and know what happened to Terry, she was the last person he would depend on to come to his aid. Reverend Anderson was guilty, his daughter so fanatic in her beliefs, that anything he said would come back to his father quicker than a boomerang.

"I warned you something would happen to Terry if you didn't try and stop him."

Despite his resolve to ignore her, he turned in

186

the swing. LuLu was hidden out of sight, only her shadow visible as she stood pressed against the exterior of the cabin.

"What do you know about Terry?"

"His father was killed in a car wreck."

"What do you know about Terry?" he repeated.

"He . . . he's in the hospital, I suppose."

"There was never a collision, LuLu. If Terry's dad's dead, he didn't die in a car wreck."

"How do you know?"

"Trust me. I know."

"But—"

"Terry's in trouble and one of us has to help him. I'd make a run for it, but I wouldn't get very far. Besides, I wouldn't even know where to start looking." He'd reacted rashly last night and had learned his lesson. From now on he would remain calm, plan his next move carefully, and say nothing to alert his dad that he knew more than he was supposed to. "Father's on the other side of the wall. I'm surprised he hasn't come out, asked who I'm talking to."

LuLu didn't answer for so long, he faced forward in the swing, positive she was gone.

"What do you want me to do, Peter?"

His heart skipped a beat. He glanced toward the window to make certain his dad was still in his favorite chair, still filling in the puzzle blanks.

"Go to Judy's cabin and make sure she's okay. Find Samantha and tell her I need to talk to her. But not to come here. I'll . . . I'll figure out a way to communicate with her later. Do you know Don Blevins?"

"The guy with crutches? Sure."

"Have you seen him?"

"Not for a couple of days. But there were so many people at the picnic and cookout that I might have missed him."

"Did you tell anyone Terry planned to sneak away to Scarletville?"

"No."

LuLu might have been a lot of things. But she was no liar.

"What else, Peter?" she asked after a moment.

"Do you think you can convince my parents they should let you see me?"

"Papa wouldn't like it if I interfered. Especially if you're being punished."

"But do you think you can do it? You're my only hope . . ."

His mother came to the door, paused long enough to pat the dyed, chestnut-colored curls over her ears, and joined him on the swing.

"Your father says it's time to come in."

He nodded, made no effort to stand. "Have you seen Mrs. Wand lately?"

"We ate lunch together yesterday."

"How's Judy?"

"Fine." She started to stand, to go back inside. She paused only when Peter made no attempt to follow. "She's fine, honey. Honest. I know it's been difficult not being able to see her. But . . ." She glanced toward the window. "Perhaps if you convince your father you're truly repentant for last night, he'll let you walk over with me later. I told Mona we'd get together and talk about what we could do to help poor Virginia Colby."

Peter's stomach churned. He was positive he was about to throw up the French toast he'd eaten for breakfast.

"Then Mr. Colby really is dead?"

"Of course, dear." His mother patted his knee. Her hand was covered with liver spots as large and reddish-brown as pennies. "You don't think your father and I would lie about something like that, do you?"

"Ter." He could barely force the name between his lips.

But his mother never had a chance to answer. Perry Elton pushed open the screen door. "Margaret, our son is being disciplined, in case you've forgotten. When I said it was time to come in, I meant now."

He followed his mother inside, apologized to his dad for not obeying sooner, and climbed the stairs to his room.

He never thought he'd see the day when he prayed that LuLu Anderson would come knocking on his door.

FOURTEEN

"Where have you been? It's nearly nine o'clock."

She ignored him until they were outside on the porch, away from earshot of his parents.

"That's the thanks I get?" LuLu stood near the steps, Bible clutched at her side, while Peter settled down on the swing. He motioned for her to sit beside him so they could speak in quiet whispers— his mom was in the kitchen, his dad in the living room—and one of them might overhear if he and LuLu talked in normal tones. But she shook her head. "Papa wouldn't approve."

He and Lucinda had more in common than he liked to admit. They both lived in fear of their father's wrath.

"You don't know the trouble I've gone to just so we could talk again." She glanced at him over the top of her glasses, brown hair draped across the side of her face. "I don't like to lie, Peter. So I stretched the truth as far as I could. And I had to make up stories to cover my tracks." She jumped, almost dropping her Bible when Margaret Elton pushed open the screen door.

"Peter, where are your manners? You haven't offered your guest anything to drink."

"Thank you, Mrs. Elton." LuLu ducked her head, stared at her scuffed brown shoes. "I wouldn't care for anything. Papa said I could only stay a little while." She looked up, smiled demurely. "Do you think Peter might walk me to my cabin? I'm a little afraid by myself after dark."

LuLu Anderson, the same girl who climbed the cliffs night after night so she could pray alone in a desolate cove, afraid of the dark? Peter wanted to laugh, the image was so ridiculous. But his mother didn't know the preacher's daughter as well as he did. She might actually fall for the ruse.

"You came over alone, didn't you? Mr. Elton's been quite lenient to let you see Peter to discuss your plans for Saturday. I'm not sure I can convince him to bend any more just yet."

"Yes, ma'am," LuLu said. "I understand. I walked over with some kids who were on their way to the clubhouse. But I'm sure I'll be safe going back. It's just that . . . well . . ." She trailed off, voice quavering, fears unspoken. Even Peter was almost convinced that she was so timid that she'd rather face the dark alone than argue with an adult.

"All right, dear." His mother stepped outside, lowered her voice to just above a whisper. "Peter, you'll come right back. I can cover with your father for ten or fifteen minutes. But you realize what'll happen if he finds out you're gone and I gave you permission?"

He nodded. "Yes, ma'am." And stood, careful that the chains made no noise. He strode quietly across the wooden porch and joined LuLu at the bottom of the stairs.

His mother was sitting on the arm of his father's favorite chair, blocking his view of the window and empty swing, when Peter looked back at the edge of the drive.

They had little time and a lot to accomplish.

"What's this about Saturday? Mother said something about plans."

"Judy's birthday." LuLu walked surefooted through the darkness, arms wrapped around the front of her sweater, Bible clutched in her left hand. "Don't ask me how I did it, but I convinced the Wands to let me give Judy a party. I told them how nice she'd been to me this summer, how we'd made plans to go to the mall once we got back to Scarletville. I told them I'd never had a close friend before. That I wanted to do something special because Judy went to so much trouble to include me in her crowd."

Judy's birthday. He'd almost forgotten, he'd been so preoccupied with other, troublesome, thoughts. He never once stopped thinking about Terry or Judy. Or gave up trying to figure out the weird conversation between his parents last night. He'd concocted countless theories, tossed them out as too bizarre, and didn't have any more clues than when he and Samantha had returned from Scarletville. Only now, he knew, wasn't the time to try and put the pieces together. He'd have lots of opportunities tonight, no doubt locked in his room, grounded for no telling how long.

"Nothing elaborate," LuLu said. "Just an intimate gathering, I told them. We'd have cake and ice cream on the porch. With their permission, of course. I told them none of us was in the mood to celebrate since Terry was in the hospital and his dad was dead, but I couldn't let Judy's eighteenth pass without—"

192

"Terry's not in the hospital." He'd told himself that so often, and believed it so strongly, that the words came out instinctively. And a bit more gruff than he had intended.

"I'm not an idiot, Peter." She slowed her pace, was close to losing her temper, too. "You've convinced me he's not in the hospital. But Mama and Papa want me to believe he is, so I pretend I do. All day long, I've said what I thought the adults want to hear so you'd have a chance to see Judy. Isn't that what you wanted?"

"Yes, LuLu. Thank—"

"I didn't do it for you. I did it for Terry. And Judy." She moved forward, worn soles shuffling through the dirt and gravel. "We'd better hurry before your dad misses you. The thing is, I told the Wands I didn't know how to plan a party. I needed help. That's where you come in. I asked your dad, and he agreed you could, but only after your mother and I begged."

"I'm surprised he gave in. He never has before." He walked in silence a few seconds. "Thank you, Lucinda."

"Save it, Peter. Right now we've got more important things to talk about. What am I supposed to do next? I've never done this sort of thing before, you know."

"Like I have?"

She ignored his sarcasm. "What are we going to do about Terry?"

"We've got to find him."

"How?"

"I wish I knew."

LuLu purposely turned left, over a grassy slope, long before she reached the narrow trail that would lead her to her door. She wanted to avoid the Colbys' cabin next door. Peter knew exactly how she felt. If they could forget he was gone, even for a few minutes, then they could pretend everything else was all right, too.

"There's another favor I need," he said. "There's a man who works here as a dishwasher. I don't know his name. But he has dark hair and drives a blue Camaro. He has something that belongs to me. Think you can find him?"

"I'll try," she answered hesitantly. "What is it I'm supposed to ask for?"

"Photographs. They're in a red binder in the backseat of his car."

LuLu stopped again, in the shadow of a tall pine tree, her face hidden in darkness. "Terry's in trouble and you're worried about snapshots of your vacation?"

"They're not pictures of the Cove. They're personal. Family . . ." He couldn't tell her about his trip to Scarletville without first explaining everything that had occurred beforehand. He'd have to tell her about Terry's determination to go, how his and Samantha's decision had been spur-of-the-moment. They'd gone only because his best friend couldn't. She wouldn't have any more idea why his house was on the market, Judy's leased to another family, than he did. He didn't want to waste time when his dad might miss him any minute. "I don't know how yet, but I think the pictures are important. I don't want to lose—"

"Never mind. I'll do it. Just tell me what I'm supposed to tell Samantha. She's worried sick because she can't talk to you herself."

"Take her with you when you go to the kitchen.

She's seen the dishwasher, she'll help you recognize him.''

"Will you stop with the stupid dishwasher already?" LuLu tromped on, only a few yards from her cabin. "Just tell me what we're going to do about Terry."

"I don't know. I asked Father a couple of times if we could go to the hospital to see him. But, of course, he said no. Terry's in intensive care and not allowed visitors.''

Lucinda slowed up again. "What if it's true, Peter? What if Terry really is hurt?''

"Mother and Mrs. Wand went to see his mother today. If Terry was in the hospital, don't you think she'd be there too?''

She paused at the end of the drive, made sure her parents weren't on the porch. "You'd better go back. I'll talk to you tomorrow.''

He took a few steps, glanced back over his shoulder. "Thanks again, Lucinda. For every—''

But she was already gone, across the yard, her long skirt billowed around her ankles as she ran through the darkness.

"I can't believe your dad let me see you." Samantha sat on the Eltons' porch swing the next morning. She held Peter's hand so tight, he was positive his fingers were bruised.

"I told Mr. Elton we wouldn't stay but ten minutes." LuLu leaned against the cedar rail at the end of the swing, arms crossed, Bible perched on the ledge within easy reach. "So you two had better talk and talk fast.''

"We went to the kitchen first thing this morning," Samantha told him. "The dishwasher doesn't come to work till this afternoon. I'll be there at three o'clock when he pulls into the employee parking lot. I'm sorry I let you forget the photo—''

''Doesn't matter,'' Peter said. ''Have you talked to Judy?''

She shook her head. ''But we'll all get a chance to see her tomorrow night. Lucinda and I talked the manager into letting his chef bake a special cake for the occasion. I think he feels guilty because he threw such a fit about the kids from Cavalier City and got her grounded.''

''My dad's going to make a freezer of vanilla ice cream,'' LuLu said. ''And Mrs. Wand said she'd serve lemonade. We're all supposed to meet at Judy's cabin after dinner, around eight o'clock.''

''I can hardly wait to hear what Judy has to say when you tell her there's another family living in her house . . .'' Samantha's voice trailed off. She looked at LuLu and back to Peter. ''You didn't tell her, did you?''

He shook his head.

''Tell me what?''

''Samantha and I went to Scarletville day before yesterday.'' He didn't have to worry his parents would eavesdrop. They'd gone to the coffee shop soon after the girls' arrival. But his dad said they'd return within twenty minutes and he wanted this tête-à-tête over before he got back. ''We didn't know we were leaving till the last minute. And we had to go that day, while everyone else was busy celebrating the Fourth.''

She was disappointed he hadn't told her before now. She'd done more than her share to help him and he'd paid her back by keeping secrets.

''I started to tell you last night. But—''

"What does Samantha mean, someone else is living in Judy's house?"

He related everything they'd found out, glancing over Samantha's shoulder to make certain his parents weren't on the trail from the clubhouse.

She stood rigid, face pale, arms wrapped around her sweater. "What about my house, Peter?"

"I don't know where you live. But we didn't go by Terry's, either."

"We came back here as fast as we could," Samantha said.

"It's better that you did, I guess." She laid her hand on her Bible, stroked the brown leather with her fingers. "The other kids who left. They didn't go home, did they? That's why no one heard from them again."

Samantha tightened her grip on Peter's hand. "Don't say that, Lucinda. Becca's my best friend."

"We have to go. I promised Mr. Elton ten minutes. If we stay longer, he won't let us come back again." She retrieved her Bible, walked to the top of the steps. "I know you're trapped, Peter. But Samantha and I aren't. Something's happened to Terry and I'm going to spend the rest of the day looking for him. He's still here, somewhere at the Cove. I know he is."

"Personally I think it's a wild goose chase." Samantha shrugged, finally let loose of Peter's hand. "But Lucinda says there's one place we haven't looked yet."

"Where?" Peter asked.

But they never had an opportunity to answer.

His parents stepped around the rear bumper of the Mercedes, his dad's soft soles crunching against the gravel as he walked toward the cabin.

"You're still talking about the party? I've known banquets that took less time to plan."

"I'm sorry, Mr. Elton." LuLu ducked her head, shuffled her feet in feigned humility. "We were just about to leave, sir."

"Thank you for letting us talk to Peter." Samantha tugged nervously at her braid. "He's been a lot of help. I wouldn't have known what to buy Judy for a present without his suggestions."

"I'm glad." He smiled, followed his wife to the door. "But it's time you came inside, son."

"Yes, sir."

He said good-bye, retreated upstairs, and closed the bedroom door behind him. He thought he might go stir-crazy if he had to stay here one more hour, much less the entire day. Judy had been grounded for over a week. How she'd managed to keep her sanity was beyond him. Peter was determined to go along with his dad's punishment, to accept it without debate. Because it was only one more day— less than thirty-six hours—before he could see Judy again. And he wasn't about to say or do anything to jeopardize sharing cake with his girlfriend on her eighteenth birthday.

"I bought this lovely charm in the gift shop for you to give to Judy." His mother sat on his bed late that afternoon. His dad was downstairs, asleep on the sofa. Normally he would have been on the golf course, but he knew his wife was too soft-hearted to make Peter stay in his room if he left them alone for a few hours.

"Thank you, Mother." Peter held the silver charm in his palm. It was small and intricate, a sun setting over a lake.

"We can't have you going to a party without a

gift." His mother stood, walked to the door. "Dinner will be ready soon. I'll call you in plenty of time."

"Mother?" He stopped her before she had a chance to leave. "Have you ever thought what it would be like to have other children?"

She patted her hair, momentarily caught off guard. "Of course. Haven't you ever wondered what it would be like to have different parents?" She returned to the bed, sat on the edge of the mattress. "I know you think we're too strict with you sometimes. Especially your father. Terry's always been given more freedom than you. But then he's been caught doing things you'd never dream. The trip to Scarletville, for example. Virginia told me Terry planned to sneak off and go with some other boys. And he would have if his father hadn't volunteered to drive him. She tried to talk Bob out of it. She didn't say, but I imagine she was concerned he'd drink and refuse to let Terry drive. If that's what caused the accident, no one's said. Not even your father. And, believe me, we'll never hear the end of it if something tragic happens to Terry too. Perry never liked Mr. Colby very much, anyway."

Peter closed his eyes, refused to believe a word she said.

Terry was okay. Safe. Somewhere here at the Cove.

Lucinda believed it and so did he.

"What made you ask such an odd question, Peter?"

He opened his eyes, looked at his mom, and shook his head. "I've had plenty of time to just sit around and think. You wouldn't believe some of the crazy questions I've asked myself."

"I'm sure that's not what your father had in mind when he grounded you. Your time might be better spent understanding why you're here and promising you won't make the same mistake again." She patted his hand, moved to the door a second time. "Some people might say I'm selfish. But I find it easier to love just one child. A mother bird misses a single egg a lot less than she would a whole nestful."

He and his dad ate dinner alone that night. His mother went to bed early, complaining of a headache.

"I heard about Terry's dad. I'm so sorry."

Peter grinned like a goon. His heart beat so fast he was afraid it would jump out of his chest and fall at Judy's feet. She'd never looked more beautiful. He pulled his chair as close to her as he could, balanced his paper plate on his knee, and didn't care the least bit that Reverend Anderson's ice cream was about to drip onto his sneakers.

"I asked if you've heard any more about Terry?"

"Huh?" He jerked himself to attention, glanced over his shoulder to determine exactly how far away the adults were from the drive. They'd allowed their children to set lawn chairs in a patch of moonlight in front of the cabin. The Wands' van was a few feet away, the dark silhouette of the hood partially obstructing his view. Samantha and LuLu ate their cake and ice cream, involved in a conversation of their own. They were excited to see Judy too but were considerate enough to allow Judy and Peter a few minutes of privacy.

"Peter?" Judy set her plastic spoon back on her plate. "What's the matter with you? Your best friend's in the hospital and you don't seem the least bit concerned. I've asked you twice if you've talked to him, or heard anything new about his condition, and all you can do is stare at me."

"Terry's not in the hospital."

"Of course he is. Mother said—"

He leaned forward, lowered his voice. "Listen to me. A lot's happened since we talked last. I only have a few minutes to fill you in. Maybe you can make some sense of it. I certainly can't. I'm grounded too, you know, and I've had plenty of time to think."

"I didn't know until Lucinda told me. What'd you do to get in trouble?"

"It doesn't matter."

"It does to me. But if you don't want to talk about it—"

"Judy, please. Listen. Samantha and I went to Scarletville. If there had been a crash, we would have seen it. Terry may be hurt. But he's not in the hospital. He's somewhere here at the Cove. There's a For Sale sign in my front yard and your house has been leased to another family. I think they plan to live there as long as your parents will let them."

"That's ridiculous. I've lived in that house all my life. Mother and Dad would never—"

"It's true," Samantha said. "I was there."

Judy turned back to Peter, ready to continue the argument. "Just how did you and Samantha happen to go to Scarletville?"

"It was Terry's idea. Only he didn't get to go. Something happened before he had a chance to leave. To Don and Virgil too, I think. No one's seen them since—''

''Who's Virgil?'' she asked.

Peter leaned forward again, tried to curb his frustration. Judy had been shut away in her cabin, she knew only what her parents told her, and he didn't blame her for asking questions. But there was no time to waste on minor details. Judy's folks had set a limit of one hour for her party. If she wasn't able to help him figure out what was going on and help him decide what to do next, he'd be forced to return to his cabin, to his locked bedroom, and might not see her again until too late. None of them were safe as long as Terry was missing. Only Judy didn't know that. And he might not be able to convince her if he couldn't tell her everything he knew.

''Peter's house was completely empty,'' Samantha said. ''Except for a photo album he found goodness knows where.'' She pointed at her straw tote bag beside her chair. ''I found it in the floorboard this afternoon. The dishwasher didn't even know it was there. Do you want it, Peter?''

''No.'' He glanced toward the cabin. His mother, Mrs. Wand, and LuLu's mom were on the porch, lighted by a single globe above the door. Their dads stood in the dim shadows of the side yard. Reverend Anderson monopolized the conversation while the other men listened and nodded politely. ''If my parents find my baby pictures, they'll know I've been to Scarletville.''

''Okay, Peter.'' Judy glanced down at her plate, her cake half-eaten, ice cream melted into a puddle of white cream. ''What does it all mean?''

''I hoped you could tell me.''

''Me? How would I know?''

"Terry's in trouble and all you two can do is argue about who should know what?" LuLu wiped her mouth on her sweater sleeve.

"We're not arguing," Peter said.

"Then somebody had better come up with a solution and quick. What can we do to help Terry?"

Judy looked at him nervously. "Peter, my hands are tied. My parents won't let me out of their sight. They've never grounded me this long before. Especially for something so minor. I think they feel guilty, sure. But only because it's my birthday and they decided to buy me a car long before Quinton's birthday."

"You're getting a car? That's really terrific . . ." Samantha's voice trailed off when she realized her congratulations were inappropriate under the circumstances.

"I may be wrong," Judy said. "But I don't think so. Dad said he has something special planned later this evening."

"What time?" Peter asked.

"I don't know. I asked why you guys couldn't stay longer than an hour. He wouldn't answer, he just acted really secretive. It has to be a car. It's the only thing I asked for."

"Excuse me." LuLu finished her cake, set her plate on the ground beside her Bible. "Do you think we could talk about Terry again? I'm sure he couldn't care less that you're getting a new car for your birthday."

Judy nodded. "You're right. I'm sorry. It's just I don't know what I'm supposed to say. Nothing makes sense. I don't know where I'll be living when I leave Sinter's Cove. A lot of the kids I've met this summer are gone and I don't know why.

Terry's supposed to be in the hospital. Only now you tell me he's not. What is it I'm supposed to do, Lucinda?''

"I don't know. But I've gone to a lot of trouble. I've even disobeyed Mama and Papa for the first time in my life. The least you can do is concentrate on Terry. He's the first guy who's ever paid any attention to me. I know you probably teased him about—''

"We didn't," Peter said. "Honest."

"Shut up and let me talk. Terrence Colby is the first guy who's ever been nice to me. I can't let anything happen to him. Samantha and I searched everywhere today because we didn't know what else to do. Peter's right. As long as Mrs. Colby's here, her son can't be far off.''

She ducked her head, the way she usually did when she walked the halls of Scarletville High. "You don't know what it's like not to have friends. Well, I've made some this summer—one in particular—and I'll be darned if I'll let anything bad happen. So unless you've got a better plan, I'm going to march right over and tell Papa everything I know. If we've moved out of the parsonage, I want to know why.''

"You can't do that," Samantha said.

"Try and stop me.''

Peter touched her arm, kept her from leaving her lawn chair. "As bad as things are, we're better off if our parents don't know we suspect anything. Don't you see? That's what got Terry in trouble. I've learned not to be impulsive. If I'd kept my mouth shut, I wouldn't be grounded. I'd be able to help you guys look for Terry.''

"You wouldn't have any more luck than we

did," Samantha said. "The only reason we think he's still here is because you convinced us. But it's like he fell off the face of the earth, like all the others. Becca disappeared from her party. So did Carl. Ann-Marie was supposed to meet me so we could celebrate her birthday. But she never showed. What makes you think Terry's going to be different? The others are gone, why shouldn't he be?"

Peter leaned back in his chair, tried to remember the exact details, every event that led up to the past disappearances. He stared at Judy so long that she began to grow uncomfortable.

"What's the matter? What'd I do?"

"Nothing." But if he was right, she was in more immediate danger than any of them imagined. Her parents had grounded her, kept her at the Cove for a reason. And not just because she'd secretly arranged for a busload of kids from Cavalier City. If they were as upset as they pretended to be, they could have easily loaded up the van and taken her back to Scarletville, the way the Cullums supposedly took their son home because they'd argued with the Wands.

His mind was made up. He knew what he had to do even if it meant he'd disobey his parents, get caught, and face a penalty far worse than being grounded.

Mona Wand came over before he had a chance to share his plans.

"It's time to open your gifts, Judy."

"Yes, ma'am." She took Peter's hand and followed her mother to the porch. She received a pair of earrings and stuffed bear from Samantha, a New Testament bound in burgundy leather from LuLu, and the silver charm from Peter. She barely had time to thank them for their gifts before Perry Elton announced that it was time to leave.

Margaret Elton smiled sympathetically at her son. "I'm sorry, Peter. Your father's right. We told the Wands we wouldn't stay past nine o'clock."

Leaving Judy was the most difficult thing he'd ever done. He couldn't even kiss her good night. She wouldn't allow it with so many other people in attendance. The Andersons were the first to leave, LuLu in tow.

Samantha waited at the edge of the drive.

"Do you mind if I walk with Peter as far as your cabin?" she asked his parents. "My curfew's not till late. I thought I'd go to the clubhouse and play videos."

Perry Elton nodded, took his wife's hand, and set out for cabin 17.

Samantha purposely lagged behind, well out of earshot. Still, she talked in a low whisper. "So, what do we do now? Judy was no help."

It was time to put his plans into action. He hated to involve Samantha, the stakes were so high, but he had to act tonight. Tomorrow might be too late.

"I lied when I said I learned not to be impulsive. But it's not like we have a lot of time, either. If we're caught—"

"Just tell me, Peter. Let me worry about the consequences."

"Find the dishwasher and tell him if he doesn't help you get your hands on a master key, you'll tell the manager he loaned us his car when he knew we weren't supposed to leave the resort. I don't care if he does work for minimum wage, he probably doesn't want to lose his job."

Samantha nodded, didn't ask why she needed a

master key or where she was supposed to find one.

"What time's your curfew?"

"Midnight. Why?"

He glanced at his watch. "It's just now nine. As soon as you have the key, go back to Judy's cabin and keep an eye on her. If her parents surprise her with a car, or keys to one, everything's okay. But if they leave the cabin, I think she's headed for trouble."

"What kind of trouble?"

"I don't know yet. But Quinton, Carl, Ann-Marie . . . They all celebrated their birthdays and we never saw them again."

"Becca, too. She was at her party one minute and gone the next. But that doesn't explain Terry. His birthday's not till next week."

"The fifteenth. Same day as mine. If I'm right, he's safe till then. But Judy's had her party." He kept his gaze fixed straight ahead in case his mom or dad slowed their pace and lingered near enough to hear the conversation. "If she leaves, follow her. The minute you know where she's going, come and get me. Let yourself in with the key and go straight to my room. You know where it is, don't you?"

She nodded.

"The door will be locked so you have to make sure the master key fits both doors."

"What do I do if your parents try and stop me? Because they will, you know, if they're home."

"If they're in bed it shouldn't be a problem. If they're awake, try not to get caught."

"Easy for you to say."

"Yeah." His dad was on the porch, key in hand. His mom leaned against the rail and waited for him to unlock the door. "The important thing is, you have to convince the dishwasher to get you the key. Otherwise I'll be locked in and won't be able to help you. Or Judy.''

''Peter,'' his dad called. ''Say good night. It's time to come in.''

He squeezed Samantha's hand. ''If I don't see you, I'll assume everything's okay. Maybe Judy will even get to tell us about her new car tomorrow.''

''I hope so, Peter.''

''Yeah. Me too.''

He was locked in his bedroom ten minutes later.

FIFTEEN

He heard the tumbler turn again at five minutes past eleven.

Samantha pushed open the door and peered through the crack. "Peter?"

He was dressed, ready to go, his jacket draped across the foot of the bed.

"I don't think your parents heard me." She glanced at the closed door across the hall. "But I had trouble getting the key to work. I was sure I made enough noise to wake them."

"They're not home. I heard them go out about ten minutes ago. I watched from my window but I couldn't see which direction." Peter swept past and hurried downstairs, Samantha in pursuit. He searched the drawers and cupboards until he found a flashlight and package of batteries beneath the sink.

Samantha was so nervous that she stood in the doorway and talked the entire time.

"The dishwasher refused to cooperate at first. Said he wouldn't help me unless I made it worth his while. I got my allowance yesterday, but not near enough to pay what he asked. So I threatened to tell the manager, just like you said. He didn't believe me, thought I was bluffing until he saw me talking to Mr. Meeker outside the kitchen doors. Of course I was just thanking him for Judy's cake, but the dishwasher didn't know that. Five minutes later we were in the basement, in the room where employees change into their uniforms. It's the room where we climbed through the window the day we came out of the cave.''

She took a deep breath, watched the front door in case his parents arrived back unexpectedly. "He jimmied open one of the off-duty security guard's lockers and took his key. Borrowed it, he said. And told me no one would miss it as long as it's back before eleven o'clock tomorrow night.''

Peter slipped the flashlight in the waistband of his jeans, the batteries in his jacket pocket.

"Did you follow Judy like I asked? Where'd she go?''

Samantha trailed behind him, past the screen door, and down the porch steps. He moved so fast, she couldn't keep pace, couldn't answer unless she shouted.

Finally, he stopped. Only because he didn't know which direction to go.

"I went back to her cabin. Just like you said. I was only there a few minutes when Judy and her parents came out. I followed them to the clubhouse and watched them go inside.''

Peter set out without waiting for the rest of the story.

"I waited a minute or two before I went in so they wouldn't suspect I was following them.'' She walked beside him as fast as she could without running. Her braid swayed from side to side. She paused occasionally to pull the strap of her tote bag back on her shoulder. "I thought they were probably headed to the restaurant or coffee shop. But I checked both places and didn't see them. The gift shop's closed. I couldn't ask the desk clerk or doorman, of course."

Peter nodded, reached the top of a grassy slope, and saw the bright lights of the clubhouse straight ahead.

"They didn't go out the back door. I'm sure. The only other place they could've gone was the basement. That's when I came to get you."

He turned south, headed across the employee parking lot to the rear of the building. The chapel, red and blue stained glass windows lighted only by a sliver of moon, was to his left, barely visible in the shadows. He found the kitchen entrance and peered inside. The chef and his assistant were near the front of the room. Everyone else—dishwasher, busboys, and waitresses—must have been out front, preparing to close.

Peter took Samantha's hand, slipped through the metal swinging door undetected, and led her through the maze of appliances and carts laden with dirty dishes. He didn't know where they were headed. Only that there had to be a stairwell from the kitchen to the basement. He couldn't chance the lobby. They might be spotted by the front office personnel or Mr. Meeker.

Samantha tugged on his hand, pointed to a grease-splattered wall just ahead.

Concrete stairs, with a rickety handrail painted bright yellow, led to the rooms below.

"Where're we going, Peter?" she whispered when they reached the lowest rung.

"You said yourself, the only other place they could've gone was the basement."

"Yeah. But why?"

"Remember the day we were in the cave?"

"Sure. I meant to tell, but never had the chance. Lucinda and I went back there when we were looking for Terry. She said that's the only other place we hadn't checked. But, of course, we didn't find him."

"Maybe you didn't look in the right place." He led the way through the maze of corridors, always alert for footsteps or voices around the next corner. There had been a shift change of security guards at eleven o'clock, and the restaurant personnel were still on the clock for another half hour, so the chances of anyone else being down here were minimal. Still, Peter couldn't afford to run into anyone unexpected and have to explain why they were here, sneaking around.

"We searched the cave," Samantha insisted. "If Terry's there, we would have found him."

Peter walked past the room with the rows of gray lockers. The door was ajar, no one inside.

"Lucinda and I split up because we thought it would save time. She went one direction, I went the other. I don't mind telling you, I was plenty scared. That place was creepy enough the first time. But at least I was with a group. I retraced our steps all the way back to where we had to climb that stupid rope. Alone, Peter. I thought for sure I'd get lost, or fall off a ledge."

"Lucinda didn't go with you?"

"No. I told you. She went the opposite direction."

"Toward her father's altar."

"Altar?" Samantha grabbed his elbow and made him stop. "What the heck are you talking about?"

He reached the end of the corridor—wished the washing machines and dryers were on so the sounds would muffle their voices—and pushed open the door to the wine cellar.

"Don't you remember? The day we heard LuLu and the Reverend talking in the cave. She thanked him because he let her see the altar again."

"Well, yeah, sure. I heard them talking. But I guess I was too scared to remember what they said."

"Judy and I discussed it afterward. I thought it a little strange . . ." He wove through the dark room, bumped into a stone wall, and knocked the flashlight from his waistband. "But I thought he just went there to pray. The way Lucinda goes to the cove every night."

"She never mentioned an altar yesterday."

He retrieved the light, turned on the switch, and trained the yellow-white beam against the wooden door at the far end of the cellar.

"Whose idea was it to split up?" he asked.

"Lucinda's."

"Whose idea was it for you to go—"

"Lucinda's," she answered before he finished. "She said we should stick to places we'd been before. That way our chances of getting lost, or hurt, were slimmer. I didn't want to go alone. But she convinced me we'd find Terry quicker if we split up."

The metal lock was unlatched as he knew it would be. He pulled open the door, shivered as dank air, as putrid as mildew, brushed against his cheeks.

Samantha slammed the door before he had a chance to enter.

"What are you saying? That Lucinda's known where Terry is all the time? That doesn't make sense. You heard her yourself. She cares about him."

He tried to open the door again, but she wouldn't let him.

"I don't much like what I'm thinking, either." He gave in, only for a moment. Judy was down here. In trouble. Lengthy explanations took time. And they had none to spare. "But it's odd how easily Lucinda convinced Mother and Father to give me a little extra freedom. You don't know them, Samantha. Always before, when I was grounded, I was allowed to see no one, no matter how much I begged. Why, all of a sudden, was Lucinda allowed to come and go as she pleased? I'll tell you. Father wanted to know what was on my mind. If I planned anything, he wanted to know well in advance."

"So Lucinda only pretended to help?"

He nodded, reached for the knob again. "I hope I'm wrong."

He held the flashlight beam at ground level and prayed he didn't lose his way before he found Judy.

He drifted in and out of consciousness the way he'd floated in the murky waters of the cove the day he banged his head and Peter had said he'd almost drowned.

He'd been here so long he'd lost track of time. He tried to count the days by remembering how many times he'd been fed. But the meals were served so sporadically, he didn't know if he was

214

eating breakfast, lunch, or dinner. But he looked forward to those times. When he was allowed to sit up, his spine supported against the rock wall, the blood flowing through his arms and legs. His wrists and ankles were bound. His eyes covered with a blindfold. He couldn't escape—not that he hadn't tried—but he managed to scoot only an inch at a time across the dirty, damp floor. And gotten so confused, even with his keen sense of direction, he was positive he'd topple into a ravine, like a sack of potatoes, and break his neck. Or worse.

He never knew who fed him. And after a while, he stopped caring.

He tried to talk, to find out everything that had happened since the night he'd climbed into the van with his dad. But no one spoke to him. No one offered him any information. He couldn't remember on his own. He'd been thrown against the dashboard an instant before the collision and the force had knocked him cold. He had a knot on his forehead just above the one he'd gotten at the cove. Memories of both events were pretty well muddled. He got a headache if he tried to remember, and rope burns if he tried to escape.

So he'd survived the best he could. Determined where he was by the sounds around him. He was in the cave where he and his friends had explored. Where he'd insisted they go, wouldn't listen when they tried to talk him out of it. Only they hadn't come this far, to this section, he was sure. The water that flowed from Lake Andrew Sinter into the mouth of the cave, and on to one of the countless streams and rivers of Wild Horse Mountain, was somewhere nearby. The water echoed constantly. He'd found the noises terrifying at first. So loud he couldn't rest. Eventually he gave in to exhaustion. And the sluicing sounds lulled him to sleep and woke him as regular as clockwork.

He had lots of time to lay in the dark and think. Heaven knew he couldn't do much else. He thought about Peter, mostly. And Lucinda. And Judy, once or twice. He remembered all the kids that had disappeared since the start of summer. And wondered if they'd gone through the same confusion and fear he experienced hour after hour. Minute by minute.

He wondered if any of them had better luck figuring out what the heck was going on. He didn't know. Even after all the scenarios he'd run through his head, like movies on the VCR, he was still pretty much clueless.

His old man was dead. Of that he had little doubt.

The air bag kept him from smashing into the steering wheel and possibly through the windshield. But he was dead. Terry felt it in his heart, a constant pain, an empty hole that wouldn't go away.

He felt something else, too. Like the candle flame he'd seen the day they ran into Lucinda and her dad in the cave. A tiny flicker of hope that wouldn't stop, wouldn't be doused no matter how often he threatened to surrender.

Peter knew he was in trouble. And Peter wouldn't give up until one of them was dead.

"Great, Ter," he thought. "Keep telling yourself that and you'll go crazy sure enough."

His best friend—the kid he'd known since kindergarten—was his only hope.

So he remained on the floor of the cave, arms

and legs bound so tight his circulation was cut off. He was gagged again after every meal, his throat so dry even sucking on a piece of sandpaper would have been a relief.

And he thought about Peter. And all the wild and wonderful plans they'd made to celebrate their birthdays.

Peter stopped. Listened. Hoped he might hear voices to guide him in the right direction.

The only sounds were Samantha's labored breathing and his own heartbeat thrumming in his chest.

"What now?" she whispered.

He didn't know. Didn't think it mattered much. They'd been so long wending their way this far— he had no idea where Judy and her parents were— that they might be too late anyway.

"No," he said aloud.

Samantha jumped at the sound of his voice and wrapped her fingers tightly around his elbow.

"No, what?" she asked.

"Never mind." He set out again, making sure the yellow beam never moved more than a few inches ahead of him. The last thing he wanted was to give away their presence. Anyone could be hiding in the pitch black ahead.

They moved a few yards, around another bend, and Samantha tightened her grip. He almost yelled. Fortunately she released her fingernails after only a few seconds.

"There's someone . . ." She spoke so quietly Peter had to stoop, his ear near her mouth, before he could hear. "There's someone behind us."

He shut off the light immediately. Pressed himself against the wall, Samantha beside him, and held his breath.

He heard footsteps. Whoever it was took a different route a few feet from where they hid.

He wasted no time. Grabbed Samantha's hand and eased back the way they'd come. He had to walk light—had to make certain his sneakers made no noise at all—and hoped Samantha knew to do the same.

There was a shadow just ahead. A silhouette. He didn't know who, only that they were going to lead him to Judy.

He stayed far enough behind not to be heard, and near enough never to lose sight of the slender shoulders and arms that seemed to be draped in a bulky sweater.

Mealtime.

Terry heard the muffled footfalls, felt the hands on his shoulder a second later. His gag was loosened and he gulped air, not caring that it was dank and tasted like the stench of mildew. Anything was a blessing after the greasy rag crammed in his mouth.

He heard the clatter of a metal plate, the clamor of silverware.

"Drink?" He'd talked so little lately, his voice sounded odd, even to himself. "I'm not hungry. Thirsty. Please."

He was given a sip of lemonade.

"Thanks. Whoever you are."

He didn't expect an answer.

And wasn't given one.

"What's for dinner? Or is it breakfast?"

He was given a bite of cold meatloaf and prayed

for more than anything that he'd get out of this mess long enough to enjoy another slice of pizza at Darby's Deli Delights.

Cold peas.

He hated peas.

And a bite of biscuit, slathered with butter.

"Another drink, please."

The lemonade was just about the best treat he'd ever known. He planned to savor the moment, enjoy the slivers of ice that melted on his tongue and dripped down his parched throat.

He ate the rest of his meal, except for the peas, and drained every drop from his glass.

"Thank you."

He was gagged again, shoved gently back on the floor and covered with a blanket. He was glad; the air in here got really cold at times.

Peter would have rushed to his best friend's rescue at once if Samantha hadn't stopped him.

She shook her head, held his arm so tightly he was positive her fingernails drew blood this time.

LuLu covered Terry with a blanket, gathered up the metal plate, eating utensils, and her Bible, and passed within a few feet of them on her way out of the secluded alcove where she'd led them ten minutes earlier.

Terry jerked in terror and began to struggle the instant Peter touched his windbreaker.

"Calm down, Ter. It's me."

He heard a groan deep in his friend's throat. A cry of pain mingled with relief.

Tears welled in Peter's eyes. He'd come close to losing his best friend, couldn't imagine everything Terry had been through in the last couple of days.

But he forced himself to remain calm. As glad as he was to be reunited, any celebrations would have to wait until later. Judy was still in danger.

He untied the gag and removed the blindfold.

Terry rubbed his eyes, blinked until he became accustomed to the dim light. "What took you so long?" His voice echoed against the rock walls.

"Shhh!" Peter clamped his hand over the boy's mouth.

Samantha reached into her tote bag, could find nothing sharper than a manicure knife tucked inside her key chain, and began to slice through the ropes that held his ankles. "What happened, Terry? How'd you wind up here?"

"I wish I knew. It all happened so quick."

"Save the explanations until later. And try to keep your voices down." Peter struggled with the cord around his wrists. The knots were too tight to manage.

"Okay. But tell me this. Who just left? They've been feeding me and trying to make me as comfortable as possible. But I'd like to know who it is so I can wring their neck."

"Lucinda," Samantha answered.

Terry swallowed hard, started to shake his head no.

"A lot's happened you don't know about, buddy." Peter slipped one knot free, and then the other. Terry rubbed his chafed flesh and flexed his fingers so his blood would circulate again. "But it's not over yet. Judy's down here somewhere and she's in trouble."

"Judy?" He lost his balance on his first attempt to stand. He sagged against Peter's shoulder, braced himself on Samantha's arm. "Where is she?

You lead the way and I'll try to follow. But don't let me slow you up.''

"I'm not letting you out of my sight," Samantha said. "I thought for sure you were dead. But not Peter. I don't know how he knew, but he swore you were okay from the minute you disappeared."

"I knew he wouldn't give up on me." Terry ventured another step, and wobbled unsteadily. "A best friend has a way of knowing these things, you know?"

"Becca." Samantha's voice quavered. "I want to believe she's still alive. That we'll find her, too. But—"

Terry reached instinctively for his ball cap. But it wasn't there. "I don't think she is, Samantha. They're all dead. Carl . . . Ann-Marie . . ."

Samantha stumbled. The woven strap slipped down her arm, her tote bag dragged on the ground. "Why? How?"

"Not important," Peter said. "Right now we've got to find Judy."

Only he didn't have the slightest idea where to start looking.

"Not that way," Samantha said. "That way leads back to the cove."

Peter was so turned around, so disoriented, that he had little choice but to trust her judgment. She'd been down here twice. And he was so shaken, so desperate to find Judy, that he didn't trust himself to make the right decisions.

"My old man's dead, isn't he?" Terry asked.

His jeans and windbreaker were streaked with grime. His reddish-brown hair was matted, his T-shirt stained with mud and perspiration. He needed a bath desperately; and insisted he walk behind Peter and Samantha so maybe they wouldn't be offended.

Peter didn't have the heart to tell him it didn't matter. They could have smelled him a quarter-mile away.

"My old man," he said again.

"No one's seen him since the day you disappeared," Peter answered.

"What about my mother? Is she okay?"

"She was in your cabin the last I saw."

"She told everyone you were in the hospital," Samantha said. "Why would she lie? Unless she thought you really were?"

Terry didn't answer. He was as much at a loss for explanations as the rest of them.

"Any idea what we're up against?" he asked Peter.

"No. Only I'm guessing you and Judy were right from the beginning."

"Our parents brought us here for a reason? Other than vacation, I mean."

Peter nodded, followed Samantha's lead. They'd passed near the wine cellar entrance a few minutes ago and were now headed in the opposite direction. Down a dark corridor he'd never ventured into before. The spaces were cramped, the rock ceilings low enough so that only Samantha didn't have to stoop. The floors were slick with mud and strewn with jagged pebbles. The air was stifling, making it difficult to breathe without coughing.

"I've been to Scarletville," he said. "My house is for sale and Judy's is leased. I couldn't imagine why until now. Our parents don't plan to go back when they leave Sinter's Cove. They're going to move somewhere else. Buy new houses. Start new lives.''

"Without us," Terry said.

"Yeah. I'm afraid so."

"You guys are so totally wrong," Samantha said. "You couldn't be further from the truth. Our parents would never . . ." She stopped. Whatever she was thinking was too unbelievable to put into words.

"So our parents want to get rid of us," Terry said. "Why?"

"Don't know," Peter answered. And didn't care. He'd find Judy, save her or die trying, and ask for explanations if he was lucky enough to survive.

His best friend slipped up beside him, draped his arm over his shoulders. "Think we ought to split up? We're likely to find her faster that way."

"No way." Samantha moved between them, forced them apart. "We're all together again and I'm not letting either of you out of my sight."

Peter led the way this time, almost positive he was headed in the only direction they hadn't searched yet. He glanced at his watch. Eleven thirty-five. His parents had been gone half an hour.

"You know," Terry said quietly. "I've had lots of time to think. I don't know what our parents are up to, what it all means, but I think it's got something to do with our birthdays."

"Today's Judy's," Peter said. "That's why we're here."

"I didn't know." He squeezed his arm consolingly. "I lost track of time. I wasn't sure what day it was."

"Thanks to Samantha, and something Judy told me after I saw her on the beach with Don Blevins,

I knew she was in trouble. Her parents told her weeks ago they had a special surprise planned for her eighteenth. But she was supposed to keep it secret. Not tell anyone. Not even me. I think that's how Becca and Carl were lured away from their parties without us knowing. They swore they wouldn't tell—not even their closest friends—they'd agreed to meet their parents somewhere secretive. I imagine they cooperated because they expected a surprise, the way Judy expects a car.''

"They got a surprise, all right," Terry said. "Only not what they'd had in mind. That's the reason I'm still here. Because it's not my turn yet. Not until the fifteenth."

"I don't believe it," Samantha said. "I still don't believe it."

"I only wish I knew why." Terry ran his fingers through his dirty hair. Now that his cap was lost, he'd developed a new habit. "I hate to ask, but if our parents want us dead, what do they hope to gain?"

"Insurance?" Samantha suggested.

"They've covered their tracks too well to risk an investigation."

"Terry's right," Peter said. "If the deaths were meant to look accidental, the police would have been notified. Someone would have come around asking questions. Remember the night of Becca's party, you asked me what all the kids here have in common? I thought you were just looking for reasons to dislike Sinter's Cove."

Terry nodded. "I'd almost forgotten, it's been so long. But, yeah."

"What do we have in common?" Samantha asked.

"None of us have brothers or sisters," Peter answered. "Not any that we know of, anyway."

"What's that supposed to mean?" Terry asked.

"Mother and Father had a strange conversation night before last. I only caught part of it. But Mother mentioned a girl named Little Meg and something about about saying good-bye to her and all the others. She also said 'each time we started a family.'"

Samantha hoisted her tote bag until the strap rested more comfortably on her shoulder. "But you just said you're her only child."

"I know it sounds crazy. But I think Mother's been through this before. Father, too."

"I gotta agree with Sam this time," Terry said. "I think you're way off base. Your parents—and maybe my mom, too—want us dead. I don't know why, and I sure as heck don't like it. But I refuse to believe my old man died trying to save my life when he had other kids and could've saved them too. I would have remembered if I had brothers or sisters."

Peter stopped. He heard footsteps. Though the cavern walls distorted sounds so well, he couldn't tell if they were ahead or behind. Samantha inhaled, held her breath. Terry shoved her off the main path, into the darkness.

"Got anything in your bag we can use as a weapon?" he whispered.

"Peter's photo album."

"'Then said I, Wisdom is better than strength . . . Wisdom is better than weapons of war.' Ecclesiastes, chapter 9."

LuLu Anderson swept through the corridor behind them, a lighted candle in one hand, a slice of

225

Judy's birthday cake on a paper plate atop her Bible in the other.

"I brought dessert," she said.

And glared at Peter.

Sixteen

Peter heard Reverend Anderson's voice somewhere ahead, as he boomed out scriptures above the roar of waters that sluiced through underground canyons.

"Judy, darling. I'm sorry." He heard Mrs. Wand's muffled wails.

"You lied to us," Samantha said.

"Yes." LuLu peered over the top of her glasses, eyes hidden by the glow of candle flame. "But I did it for your own good."

"By pretending to help? You knew where Terry was all the time."

Peter didn't wait around to argue. He climbed the slippery incline, letting the echoes of Reverend Anderson's sermon guide him. The flashlight was directed straight ahead because he no longer cared if anyone saw him coming. Judy was here, so close he heard her voice and knew she was crying.

His mother saw him first. Opened her mouth to cry out. But not before his father saw him, too.

Reverend Anderson glanced up, closed his Bible, and set out for the footbridge that spanned over the river, across the two cliffs.

"Waymon." Perry Elton strode ahead of the

other man, his gaze fixed solidly on his son. "Let me handle this."

Peter froze. Thought he'd know what to do once he found Judy. But the sight of his parents—his mother wrapped in her knitted shawl, his father in the trousers and white shirt he'd wear to the office—shocked him so much, he could only stand and stare.

He didn't know what he'd expected. A convent of satan worshippers, perhaps. His parents dressed in black capes, Judy stretched across the Reverend's altar, offered up like a sacrificial lamb.

But his mom and dad, and the dozen other people gathered around them, behaved as casually as if they'd gotten together for a night of pinochle.

"How did you get here, son?"

His father's voice—the kind he usually reserved for mealtime when he wanted to discuss Peter's failing grades or the fact that he'd left the lawn mower out in the rain again—stirred him to action. He took in the surroundings as quickly as he could, regained his courage, and descended a series of steps carved into the rock wall. He paused at the edge of another sharp drop-off and the onset of the swinging bridge that kept him from Judy. He couldn't see her yet, but he knew she was there. She'd stopped crying except for an occasional frightened sniffle.

"I asked you—"

"I heard you, Father." His voice echoed through the wide open spaces. This grotto was larger than any he expected after the tight squeezes and cramped corridors he'd been through. He averted his gaze long enough to gauge the water that flowed beneath the bridge. No way could he, or anyone else, suffer a fall that far and survive. The ropes and wooden slats looked too weathered, too rickety to support his weight. But he ventured ahead anyway. The first plank creaked and sagged beneath his shoes.

"Stay there, Peter," his father said. "I'll come across."

"No." He couldn't allow his dad to gain the upper hand. Couldn't let himself be bullied or intimidated. He'd come this far and couldn't back down now. He took another step, determined to reach the other side before his dad could stop him. The bridge swayed left. He almost lost his balance.

"Peter, I don't know what you think you're doing. But I want you to stay right where you are." Perry Elton stepped onto the opposite end, grabbed the ropes with both hands, and moved ahead surefooted and confident.

He stopped only when he saw Terry, Samantha, and LuLu at the top of the cliff.

"You shouldn't have come, son. None of you should be here."

Terry scaled the stairs, walked to the end of the bridge. "Well, we did. So whatever's going on, it's over."

Perry Elton took another step. "What is it you think's going on?"

"Kidnapping, for starts. And murder, too, I guess."

"Murder? Who's been killed?"

"My old . . . my dad."

"Your father was killed in a car accident." He nodded to the group of people behind him, to Mrs. Colby in particular. "If you don't believe me, ask your mother."

She stood beside Peter's mom, red hair draped around her face and shoulders. She refused to look up, to confront her son.

"What about Becca, my best friend?" Samantha was still on the top step, tote bag slung over her shoulder.

"What about her?" Perry Elton asked.

"Where is she?"

"Home, I suppose."

"You're lying."

He shook his head. Took another step. "I haven't talked to the Kings since they left. None of us have."

"Why'd she leave so quick, without even saying good-bye?"

"You'll have to ask her. When you see her again."

"I won't be seeing her and you know it. Chances are someone else has moved into her house by now."

He stopped, steadied himself against the ropes. "How do you know that?"

"I know."

"We've been to Scarletville," Peter said. "I talked to the woman who's living in Judy's house."

His father failed to move forward. So Peter eased across the bridge, one step at a time, the planks sagged beneath his feet, the ropes wavered unsteadily in his hands. He didn't dare look down, didn't want to see the water roiling beneath him. One wrong move, one unexpected jerk of the bridge from his dad and he could easily go sliding off into the pool below.

He felt the boards behind him bounce, glanced

back in time to see LuLu take her first few tentative steps. Terry was behind her, trying to stop her from going any further.

"Peter . . ." She clutched her Bible against her chest. "Let me talk to you."

"No. Go back."

"Let me explain why I didn't tell you about Terry."

"Go back, LuLu."

But she was in the center of the bridge, close enough to touch his shoulder and near enough so she could talk so that his father wouldn't overhear the conversation.

"What time is it?" she asked.

He wanted to laugh, the question was so inappropriate.

"What time?" she asked again.

He glanced at his watch, had a difficult time seeing in the dim light. "Almost midnight. Ten minutes till."

"I don't think they'll hurt Judy while we're here. But I can't be sure. You've got to think of a way to keep 'em distracted for at least ten minutes."

"Why should I do anything you say? I trusted you once and you let me down."

"I can give you my reasons. Or we can help Judy and talk about it later."

He nodded, glanced at his dad halfway between him and the other end of the bridge. "What'll I do? What'll I say?"

"Anything. As long as you keep him talking until—"

"Daughter!" Reverend Anderson hurried up behind Perry Elton. The footbridge rocked side to side. LuLu's hands slipped and her left leg splayed

231

out. One brown shoe slid from her foot, went spiraling to the river below.

"Stay back, Papa!"

"Lucinda, you have broken every vow you've ever made to your mama and me. Your disobedience is a sin and I won't tolerate it. Come across at once."

"No, Papa."

"I said—" He stomped forward, tried to wrest his way past Peter's dad, but there wasn't room. The bridge swayed out of control again.

Peter grabbed the ropes, felt his sneakers sliding out from under him.

LuLu held on to his shoulders, for support he thought, until he looked back in time to see her climb over the rope rail and teeter dangerously close to the edge.

"What the hell are you doing, Lucinda?" Terry shouted.

"I'll jump, Papa. I swear I will!"

"Daughter. Please. Calm down."

Peter reached for her arm, to pull her back to safety. But she shrugged out of his reach, only the heel of her shoe still braced against the wooden planks.

"If I fall, Papa, I'll die. And it'll be too bad for you and Mama because I'm not eighteen yet. Isn't that the way it works? If I die before my next birthday, then all the lies you've told, all the efforts you made to bring me here have been for nothing. I may be wrong, Papa. Tell me if I'm wrong."

He gripped his Bible so tightly that his knuckles turned pale. "No, daughter. You're not wrong."

"Then back away. All the way off the bridge. Mr. Elton, too."

Both men obeyed. Though Peter was certain his father was so determined to have his way, he'd charge at them at the last minute, and LuLu would lose what little grip she managed to hold on to. The reverend's daughter could fall, and it wouldn't matter. It was Peter he wanted to get his hands on.

"What time is it?" LuLu asked.

He turned, his back to his dad, and looked at his watch. "Eight minutes."

"You can't hold on that long." Terry was at the end of the bridge, about to walk across to where Peter leaned against the slack ropes.

"Peter, darling." It was his mother's turn to appeal to him. She stood where his father had been moments before. "You have to understand . . ."

"Understand what, Mother?"

"Your father and I love you. Truly we do."

He hated to think where he'd be if they hated him.

"Like you loved Little Meg?" he shouted.

She clutched at her shawl in time to keep it from sliding off her shoulders. "How do you know . . . ?"

"There have been others, too," he said. "How many more, Mother?"

She looked at her husband, tears in her eyes. "We loved them all, each and every one."

LuLu tried to climb back over the ropes, but couldn't manage alone. The bridge swayed and creaked each time she moved.

"How many, Mother?"

She shook her head. "Peter, you have to understand. It seemed so right in the beginning. I was young, and beautiful, and your father so handsome. We had our whole lives ahead of us. Having a child was really the furtherest thought from our minds. I mean, we were already married and we hadn't even talked about children. I was so in love I didn't think it possible to have room in my heart for anyone else. Not even a baby. Especially not a baby. Life was so wonderful and I was so selfish. When I discovered it could go on forever, that nothing had to change, I jumped at the chance. I never dreamed holding your child in your arms was so much more wonderful. That it was worth dying for. But it was too late by then. Your father and I had already . . ."

"Already what, Mother?"

He glanced at his watch. He didn't know what was supposed to happen at midnight. But it was five minutes away.

"We were too late, Peter. We'd already made up our minds. And there was nothing we could do to change them."

"You could have," he said. "And you probably would have if Father hadn't talked you out of it."

She started to shake her head no. "I told you, we were young. Only a few years older than you. We were on our honeymoon the first time we came here. Back then, it was an adults-only resort. No children allowed. Mostly singles. A few newlyweds like us." She smiled at the memories. "That's why I still say Sinner's Cove, that's what people used to call it. We returned every year on our anniversary. That's how we met the Colbys, Merl and Jolene Cullum, and the Owensbys."

Peter closed his eyes for just a second. Tried to imagine his parents as young and so desperate to hang on to their happiness at any cost.

"You met them. And talked them into making the same decision as you and Father."

"No." She shook her head vehemently. Brown hair tinged with gray fell across her forehead. "Your father and I thought we were the only ones. We never shared our secret, we never even discussed it among ourselves. I never told him, but I felt so guilty, I decided we'd never have children. The solution seemed so simple."

"But you did, didn't you? Have a baby."

"Yes. I found out I was expecting shortly after our third vacation. Weeks later I received a letter from Virginia sharing the same news. Only there was something sad in her letter. So I called her. And that's when I discovered she and Bob had made the same bargain with Andrew Sinter that your father and I had."

He glanced at his watch. Three minutes.

"Go on. Tell me what happened."

"I had my baby, of course. And raised him to age eighteen, just like I'd promised."

"And brought him back here for his birthday."

"Yes."

"Only he never went home, did he? Just like I'm not supposed to leave."

"I had no choice. I had your father to consider, too. I'd made promises to him. I couldn't just back out because I felt guilty . . ."

LuLu was safely back across the rail. She leaned against Terry's shoulder as he led her toward the cliff.

Two minutes.

Samantha waited until LuLu was on solid ground before she ventured across the wooden slats. She balanced herself with both hands, the strap of her tote bag sliding down her shoulder with every step.

When she was directly behind Peter, she dropped

her bag, reached inside, and pulled out the photo album.

"I'm sorry I looked, Peter. But I couldn't help myself. I was just so curious what you looked like as a baby. But really, how could you believe they were you? Most of the pictures look nothing like you do now."

His mother recognized the red binder. Fresh tears spilled down her wrinkled cheeks. "Where'd you get that?"

"It's the only thing left, Mother. Everything else is gone."

"Not gone, Peter. Just moved. But I guess you already know that."

"I guess I do."

Sixty more seconds.

He handed Samantha the flashlight, opened to the first page of the album and ripped out the black and white photograph of his parents with a baby in his mother's lap.

"Boy or girl?"

"Boy," his mother said. "We called him Perry Bob until he started school. After that he insisted we call him by his given name. Robert."

He tossed the picture off the side of the bridge, didn't wait until it hit the river before he tore out the next. One of a little girl with long, curling eyelashes.

"Little Meg?"

His mother nodded. "You would have liked her, Peter. The two of you have so much in common."

"This has gone on long enough, Margaret." Perry Elton took his wife's arm and gently led her from the bridge. "You're only torturing yourself.

I'm not sure how much more I can take, either. The Wands—''

"The Wands have decided to let their daughter go." Judy's dad walked with her from the crowd, past Reverend Anderson and the Owensbys, his wife close behind. Judy was too shaken up to look at Peter, too scared to break free of her father's grasp.

"Don't be a fool," Reverend Anderson said.

"Shut up, Waymon. Each time is harder than the time before. It's not worth it anymore."

Twelve seconds. If his watch was right.

"We told ourselves it didn't matter," Mr. Wand said. "Our children would only grow up, get old, and die anyway."

Five seconds.

"Mona and I have lived long enough. Now it's our daughter's turn."

Midnight.

Judy screamed as her father pitched forward— she made a grab for his sleeve but missed—before he hit the ground. Her mother collapsed too, gasped for air, and rolled face first on the muddy floor. Peter took a few running steps before his sneakers slid out from under him. He dropped the photo album, landed on his back, and thought for sure he'd never breathe again. The bridge rocked and rolled beneath him like some crazy carnival ride out of control. In a few more seconds he'd be swept off the edge, with nothing to catch him but the river.

"Peter." Judy slipped her arm through his and helped him stand. "They're dead, Peter, and I'm going to be too if I don't get out of here." She was crying, long black hair stuck to her face and tangled around her shoulders. "Your parents have to keep you alive until your birthday. You and Terry and LuLu . . . But not me. They know I'll tell if I make it out of here alive."

Peter's father, Reverend Anderson, and Samuel Owensby were on the bridge, one behind the other, walking as fast they could while they held on to the ropes.

He looked back only once. And saw the reverend's altar. A boulder twice as large as any in the cove, so smooth and polished it glistened like onyx.

His mother was on her knees beside Judy's mother. She shouted at his father, a last-minute anguished plea to save their son. For her sake, if nothing else.

"I sent Samantha and Lucinda on ahead." Terry met them at the base of the rock steps. "I told them to lock the cellar door and not let anyone out unless they were sure it was us."

"We'll never outrun 'em," Judy said.

"Sure we will."

"We have to." Peter reached the top of the stairs behind the others. He'd lost track of his flashlight, hoped Samantha had it, and prayed she and LuLu were far enough ahead that they'd escape even if he failed to.

Perry Elton was the first to reach the cliff, the first to climb two steps. He glanced up, smiled at Peter briefly, the way he had only once or twice before. When he was especially proud of his son. He turned back and blocked the other mens' paths.

"You'll have to go through me first, gentlemen. And I'm sure you know you'll have one heck of a fight on your hands."

Peter never saw his dad again. But he lived with

the memories that Perry Peter Elton III came through for his only child when it mattered most.

"I knew something was going on since my first night at the Cove." Lucinda rode in the passenger seat, her Bible clutched securely in her lap.

Terry was behind the wheel of Samantha's parents' car. Samantha, Peter, and Judy were jammed in the backseat.

Judy hadn't spoken since they'd climbed inside and Samantha dug in the bottom of her tote bag until she found the keys. She'd stared out the window, cried a few times, and refused to answer when Peter asked if she wanted to go to a hospital. No one mentioned her parents, none of them dared ask if she'd seen too how quickly they'd aged before they'd died. Her father's hair was gray, her mother's skin as pale and brittle as crepe paper.

"I followed Rebecca that night, during her party," Lucinda said. "I was going to read to her from the Bible. Talk to her if I could. She seemed so . . ."

"Becca was a little wild at times." Samantha fought back tears. "I remember once she told me she felt distanced from her parents, and did the things she did just to get their attention. She could hardly wait to turn eighteen so she could move away from home. Maybe then they'd miss her, she said."

"I lied," Lucinda went on, "when I told you I heard her argue at the cove. I saw her meet her parents at the clubhouse. She was really mad that they insisted she leave the party. She wanted to go back, but they wouldn't let her. I followed them to the basement. I don't know why. I guess because

I was fascinated by Becca, she's so different from me, and I wanted to make friends with her. I had decided this summer was going to be different, that I was going to hang around with the kind of kids who wouldn't be caught dead talking to me at Scarletville High.

"I didn't find the cellar door or caves until the next day. That's when I found Papa at his altar. He was angry that I'd followed him. But I convinced him that I didn't, that I'd run into him by accident. He told me he came there each day to pray. And I should find my own quiet spot to do the same. But I must never, ever tell anyone about his altar. Especially not any of the young people."

"Did you ask why?" Terry asked.

"He said some of the parents had asked him to counsel their children. Some of them, like Becca, were out of control. He agreed to help, but only if he could do it his way. That meant bringing them to the cave, without their friends knowing, so he could talk to them in private. I was so proud of Papa for giving up his vacation to continue his work that I promised not to tell. That's why I stopped you the day you were down there exploring. I was afraid you'd find the altar by accident, the way I did, and ruin everything Papa had accomplished so far. I didn't suspect the truth until much later. I thought the kids who left went home, to try and start over with their parents, the way Papa said."

"That doesn't explain how Becca's nose ring got at the cove," Terry said.

"I think she must have tried to escape and made it that far."

"I don't know how. The crosscurrent's so strong—"

"I guess anything's possible when you're swimming for your life," Samantha said.

"But why'd you lie to us about Terry?" Peter asked.

She turned in the seat, as far as her shoulder strap would allow. "Papa said he was being punished for trying to run away. I told him it was cruel and I wouldn't let him do it. He said Terry wasn't the only one, that there were two other guys. Their parents were so upset that his counseling had failed, they decided to try their own methods. He said if I told anyone, I'd jeopardize their safety. That he could no longer be responsible for what might happen."

"So Don and Virgil are all right?" Terry asked. "Where are they?"

"Since their parents are still at Sinter's Cove . . . I guess they are, too." She turned back, stared out the passenger side window. "I didn't know Judy was in so much danger tonight. Honest. If I'd known, I would have told someone. I never dreamed Papa . . ." Her voice trailed off.

No one spoke for several minutes.

"I guess no one's going to bring it up, so I will." Terry gripped the steering wheel tightly, swung off the road onto the ramp that would take them to the interstate and the nearest sheriff. "Our parents sold their souls to the devil? Is that what happened?"

"In a way," Peter said from the backseat. "But I'm not sure the devil has anything to do with it. Or their souls either, for that matter."

241

"Thanks, buddy, that really answers my question."

"There are no answers," LuLu said. "At least not the kind we're likely to understand. Peter's mother said she was young, and beautiful, and the happiest she'd ever been the first time she came to Sinter's Cove. On her honeymoon. She said she wanted life to go on exactly as it was. So that's what happened. Our parents traded one thing for another. Only it was with Andrew Sinter, not the devil."

"They traded their children for . . ." Samantha leaned forward so she could try and see through the dim light. "For what?"

"Eternal youth," LuLu said. "Beauty. Happiness."

"So Sinter's Cove is like the Fountain of Youth?" Terry asked.

"That's a myth, a fable." Judy spoke for the first time. "Our parents meant to kill us." She rested her head on Peter's shoulder and closed her eyes. "Nothing else matters."

None of them knew what to say. And remained quiet for several miles.

Terry finally glanced in the rearview mirror and caught Peter's attention. "Doesn't anyone besides me want to know how?"

"How what?"

"How they planned to kill us? Throw us into the river? Drink our blood? What?"

"Do you really want to know?" Lucinda asked.

"No." He looked at his best friend again. "I guess I don't."

EPILOGUE

Nine Months Later

Seventeen-year-old Charmel Scofield was forced to quit her part-time job at St. Anthony's Hospital the month before final exams at Whitman High School because her algebra grades had fallen well below average and her parents insisted she couldn't keep up her studies and work too.

Charmel hated to leave, not because the pay was great, or she'd miss roaming the halls and being assigned tasks none of the other personnel liked to tackle, but because she liked meeting new people. Especially the expectant mothers on the third floor, west wing, where she worked one afternoon a week. She'd asked to be assigned there permanently, but continued to be rotated from floor to floor, each day a different assignment.

She glanced at the clock above the nurses' station. She'd been off duty five minutes, her farewell party had been short but sweet, and there was nothing left to do but grab her purse from the closet and go downstairs to the parking lot. Her dad had no doubt arrived on time. He was such a stickler for details. And he'd be irritated and in a bad mood if he had to wait. The last thing she wanted to hear tonight was how irresponsible she was. Charley Scofield liked to remind her of that every chance he got.

She grabbed the bouquet of flowers and Mylar balloons her supervisor, Mrs. Paine, had given her, and headed to the elevators in the fourth floor lobby.

"Wait up, Charmel. I'll walk with you."

Mrs. Paine was a tall brunette who'd dedicated her life to the medical profession. She'd worked at St. Anthony's for twenty-two years.

"Where're you headed?" Charmel asked.

"Third floor. Second floor. And all the way to the pharmacy in the basement." She slapped several manila folders against her palm. "I promised a dozen people they'd have these files an hour ago. Oh well, what do they expect when the computers go off-line constantly?"

"Yeah," Charmel said and pushed the down button.

"We're sure going to miss you around here. Think your folks will let you come back once your grades are up to par?"

"I'm not sure." She stepped inside the car when the metal doors slid open. "But I have all summer to convince them. We're going on vacation, just the three of us, for the first time I can remember."

"Wonderful." Mrs. Paine ran her fingers over her lips, a habit she had, though she rarely wore makeup. "I hope you have a good time."

"Mom says we will. She has something extra special planned for my birthday."

The elevator stopped on the third floor and the doors slid open.

"Want me to deliver your files here?" Charmel asked. "I planned to stop and say good-bye anyway."

"Thank you, dear." Mrs. Paine handed her the top three folders. "As I said, I'm going to miss you. You're always so helpful."

Charmel strode toward the west wing as fast as she could. Her dad would really be antsy by now. She hoped he'd understand, not that he'd give her much chance to explain. Patience was not in his vocabulary.

She paused outside the nursery window where the newborns were placed so visitors could get their first look. There were three babies tonight, one girl and two boys.

And only one proud parent standing before the glass, beaming down at his offspring.

"Which one's yours?" she asked.

"There," the dark-haired man pointed. "Second from the left."

Charmel leaned nearer and read the name plate above the infant's head.

"Tyrone. Boy. What'd you name him?"

"Carlton Dewayne."

"That's cute. Is he your first?"

"Yes," the man said. "My one and only."

SPINE-TINGLING SUSPENSE FROM AVON FLARE

NICOLE DAVIDSON

THE STALKER	76645-0/ $3.50 US/ $4.50 Can
CRASH COURSE	75964-0/ $3.99 US/ $4.99 Can
WINTERKILL	75965-9/ $3.99 US/ $4.99 Can
DEMON'S BEACH	76644-2/ $3.50 US/ $4.25 Can
FAN MAIL	76995-6/ $3.50 US/ $4.50 Can
SURPRISE PARTY	76996-4/ $3.50 US/ $4.50 Can
NIGHT TERRORS	72243-7/ $3.99 US/ $4.99 Can

THE BAND
by Carmen Adams 77328-7/ $3.99 US/ $4.99 Can

EVIL IN THE ATTIC
by Linda Piazza 77576-X/ $3.99 US/ $4.99 Can

BACK FROM THE DEAD
by Carol Gorman 77433-X/ $3.99 US/ $4.99 Can

THE LAST LULLABY
by Jesse Osburn 77317-1/ $3.99 US/ $4.99 Can

⇒TERRIFYING TALES OF⇐ SPINE-TINGLING SUSPENSE

THE MAN WHO WAS POE   Avi
71192-3/ $4.50 US/ $6.50 Can

DYING TO KNOW   Jeff Hammer
76143-2/ $3.50 US/ $4.50 Can

NIGHT CRIES   Barbara Steiner
76990-5/ $3.50 US/ $4.25 Can

CHAIN LETTER   Christopher Pike
89968-X/ $3.99 US/ $5.50 Can

THE EXECUTIONER   Jay Bennett
79160-9/ $4.50 US/ $5.99 Can

THE LAST LULLABY   Jesse Osburn
77317-1/ $3.99 US/ $4.99 Can

THE DREAMSTALKER   Barbara Steiner
76611-6/ $3.50 US/ $4.25 Can

Look for All the Unforgettable Stories by Newbery Honor Author

★ AVI ★

THE TRUE CONFESSIONS OF CHARLOTTE DOYLE
71475-2/ $4.50 US/ $5.99 Can

NOTHING BUT THE TRUTH   71907-X/ $4.50 US/ $5.99 Can

THE MAN WHO WAS POE   71192-3/ $4.50 US/ $5.99 Can

SOMETHING UPSTAIRS   70853-1/ $4.50 US/ $6.50 Can

PUNCH WITH JUDY   72253-4/ $3.99 US/ $4.99 Can

A PLACE CALLED UGLY   72423-5/ $4.50 US/ $5.99 Can

SOMETIMES I THINK I HEAR MY NAME
72424-3/$3.99 US/ $4.99 Can

———————— *And Don't Miss* ————————

ROMEO AND JULIET TOGETHER (AND ALIVE!) AT LAST
70525-7/ $3.99 US/ $4.99 Can

S.O.R. LOSERS   69993-1/ $4.50 US / $5.99 Can

WINDCATCHER   71805-7/ $4.50 US/ $6.50 Can

BLUE HERON   72043-4 / $3.99 US/ $4.99 Can

"WHO WAS THAT MASKED MAN, ANYWAY?"
72113-9 / $3.99 US/ $4.99 Can